THE LIBRARY
OF DEATH

THE LIBRARY OF DEATH

Ronald S. L. Harding

With an Introduction by

John Pelan

RAMBLE HOUSE

ISBN 13: 978-1-60543-576-3

ISBN 10: 1-60543-576-7

Cover Art: Gavin L. O'Keefe
Preparation: Fender Tucker

DANCING TUATARA PRESS #20

THE MYSTERIOUS MR. HARDING

The list of British thriller authors from the 1930s includes a number of skilled yet nearly forgotten authors who specialized in treading the ground between the overtly supernatural and those that featured a rationalized explanation of events. Included in this small but illustrious group are Walter S. Masterman, James Corbett, Arlton Eadie, and Ronald S. L. Harding. While both Masterman and Corbett wrote a number of straightforward mysteries, their most intriguing novels are those that kept the reader guessing as to whether or not supernatural forces are actually at work. These novels were paralleled in the U.S. by the "weird menace" magazines typified by *Horror Stories, Terror Tales* and *Dime Mystery Magazine;* where authors such as Arthur J. Burks, Wyatt Blassingame, and John H. Knox were the standard-bearers of the genre. Without a similar venue, the British authors focused on full-length novels as opposed to the novella or novelette of the prevalent in the U.S.

Splendid examples of this type of yarn include Masterman's *The Green Toad* and *The Curse of Cantire* and Corbett's *Vampire of the Skies.* However, the one author who truly excelled at this type of novel was Ronald S.L. Harding. Little information on Harding is available, and his books are at least as scarce as those of contemporaries such as Mark Hansom and R.R. Ryan.

Whereas the U.S. had the pulp magazines, the market in the U.K. was quite different, with the thriller novels being marketed primarily to the lending libraries. While this strategy generated a wide readership it also accounts for the scarcity of these titles. One of the unfortunate circumstances of this program was the fact that books were literally read to pieces; another factor was the library policy of immediately removing and tossing out the dust jackets of all new arrivals. Some publishers, such as Wright & Brown produced a sturdy if plain product that held up to the multiple readings. Ronald

S. L. Harding had the misfortune to be published by London's Modern Publishing Company, an imprint known for both their volume of titles and the shoddiness of their product.

Were these conditions not enough to ensure the survival of only a very few copies of Harding's books an even more devastating circumstance was the bombing of the warehouse district during the blitz. In some cases, entire print runs were destroyed; (the author of *Dark Sanctuary,* H.B. Gregory told me that of the 400 copies printed of his classic horror novel the only copies that survived were his personal copies (3) and perhaps a dozen or so copies that had been mailed to reviewers in Canada and Australia.)

We have been fortunate enough to secure copies of two of Harding's novels and with luck, we ought to be able to track down at least a couple more of the half-dozen novels known to exist.

The Library of Death begins at a leisurely pace, and a tone that seems to set the stage for a light romance. Harding deftly builds the mystery and from the moment we learn of the legend of a headless spectre that purportedly stalks the grounds and rumors of hereditary vampirism the novel undergoes another transformation with the light tone of the early chapters forgotten as horror is piled upon horror. . .

Harding handles these transformations with a sure hand drawing the reader along a path that leads from the prosaic into a setting where not only does the supernatural appear to be possible, but probable.

The novels of Ronald S. L. Harding are long overdue for rediscovery my modern readers and with the publication of *The Library of Death* and its companion volume, *One Dreadful Night* Dancing Tuatara Press has taken the first steps in introducing the works of Ronald S.L. Harding to a new generation of readers.

John Pelan
Midnight House
Gallup, NM

THE LIBRARY OF DEATH

CHAPTER I

"COME ON, JOHN, we've got the whole afternoon to our-selves. He'll not be back till late. Hooray!"

And Elsie Mervyn hurled her tennis racquet high into the air, catching it again as it fell to earth, with a joyous laugh.

She rushed across the lawn towards a young man in white flannels who was walking slowly towards her, miscalculated the distance between them, and, quite unable to check herself in time, bumped into him with a force that nearly knocked him over.

"There now," she panted, recovering her balance with an effort, "I nearly knocked you down! What a dreadful tomboy you must think me!"

John Tarren looked steadily into her laughing eyes with an expression in his own peculiar to young men very much in love, and replied: "I think you are the most beautiful thing I have ever seen!"

"Compliments again! What a flatterer you are! Well, I wasn't fishing, anyway, so my conscience is clear!"

"You've no need to fish," replied John. "Who could help stating facts? Look in the glass one day and see for your-self!"

Elsie laughed, blushed, and murmured something about "idle flattery." Then she suggested that they should get on with their game of tennis.

Tarren had certainly not exaggerated when he had said that Elsie Mervyn was beautiful. She really was a sight well calculated to make any man's blood spin round the quicker. With her golden hair unbobbed, and worn picturesquely braided and rolled into "earphones" on either side of her lovely face: her great speaking eyes: her delicately tinted cheeks: her voluptuous lips: full-bosomed rounded figure: soft white dimpled arms: and kissable hands.

She was the one ray of sunshine in the whole of the gloomy, isolated, rambling, old Manor house which is the scene of our story. Her step-father, Sir Charles Dorsay, Bart., was its master, and, as he was a widower of well over sixty, Elsie could hardly help having a pretty lonely life of it as practically the only young girl in the little village in which "Dorsay Hall" stood, surrounded by some half a dozen acres of land, in dismal and solitary state.

When Sir Charles had engaged young John Tarren as his secretary, Elsie welcomed him as someone of her own age, tastes, and education; and it had not been long before the two young people had become inseparable companions.

But John looked upon Elsie as something more than a companion. He had loved her passionately from the first moment he had set eyes on her on that day of days when he had been summoned to interview her step-father. He had been conducted to the library by the butler, there to wait the pleasure of the master of the house. He had been compelled to wait quite a time, and it was during this long and anxious ordeal that Elsie had presented herself.

She just ran into the library from the garden to restore a book she had been reading to its place, had been unable to reach the shelf, and, of course, Tarren had come to her res-cue. From that very moment he had adored her, and fate had been kind enough to intervene on his behalf by prompting Sir Charles to see in young John Tarren the very thing he was looking for.

And so, when he moved into "Dorsay Hall," John did so with feelings much akin to those of Romeo climbing Juliet's balcony. There was one important difference however—his Juliet had yet to be woo'd and won.

And how terribly difficult it was to start that all-important wooing too in spite of the numerous opportunities which pre-sented themselves. Always like an invisible barrier between John and his heart's desire was the knowledge that she was an heiress, and that he had not a single prospect in life beyond the beggarly £100 a year which Dorsay paid him besides his keep.

True, his father had been an officer of high rank in the Indian army: but he had come badly to grief financially just after the war, and at his death—which happened a year before this story opened—John had been forced to leave Oxford without taking his degree and go out into the world to earn his own living as best he could.

So how could he ask Elsie to be his wife when he had nothing to offer her save love? He felt that he dare not confess the state of his feelings lest she should think him a vulgar fortune hunter, and that warm, friendly, glow leave her clear eyes, to be replaced by coldness—or, perhaps, even by scorn.

He felt he would rather keep silent, and dream in his imagination that she loved him just a little, than run the risk of having every illusion dispelled. Better deceive himself into a little hope, than take a fifty-to-one chance of materialising a sweet dream, with utter despair as the probable issue.

Besides—even if she should happen to return his love—there would be that ancient lovers' dragon to contend with—the "old man!" Tarren knew perfectly well that an utterly penniless secretary was the very last person in the world Sir Charles would choose as a suitor for his step-daughter's hand. He knew, further, that should it come out that he even dreamed of such a thing he would at once be dismissed.

And dismissal would mean banishment from the one person in the world he most wished to be near.

And, although Dorsay gave every sign that he objected even to their friendship, yet they found plenty of opportunity of being in each other's company, since the old man spent much of his time away from home. There was an excellent tennis-lawn, and, since Tarren was a first-class player, Elsie welcomed him as a partner.

On this particular summer's day on which our story opens, Sir Charles had gone off to London to see his solicitor, and would not return before late that night. So Elsie and

John, who were, by now, pretty close friends, thoroughly enjoyed their game.

"If you look at me all the while, and not at the ball," called out Elsie to John, after she had won her third game in succession with amazing ease, "you'll never hit it at all! Look out! It's coming over!"

She gave the ball a smart blow with her racquet, and sent it spinning across the net to John, who caught it at rather an awkward angle, and sent it back at top speed. It soared high over the net, a good thirty yards or more from where Elsie was standing, and she dashed after it. As luck would have it she stumbled, caught her foot in a hole in the lawn, and fell headlong.

John was at her side in an instant. "You're not hurt?" he asked anxiously.

"Nothing to speak of. Just twisted my ankle a bit."

She tried to get up, but could not manage it.

John stooped down, and, putting his strong arms round her, picked her up like a child.

For one brief moment her soft body, warm and pulsating, was pressed against him, and the touch of her dispersed all his months-old self-restraint like a fire would a snowball.

Every impediment and convention melted, and the next thing John knew was that he had gathered Elsie right into his arms, crushing her to his madly-beating heart like a famished rattlesnake would its prey, and feeding his starving lips with long, passionate kisses the vehemence of which nearly smothered him.

He kissed her eyes, her hair, her neck, her breast, and then again sealed her mouth with his own—presumably to stifle any remonstrances.

But somehow or other none came, and so he started all over again: this time with the added joy of feeling her cling to him and return his kisses.

In one second of delirium he knew that she loved him too. He had thrown the dice and won!

Elsie was blushing from head to foot, when, at last, John stopped kissing her from sheer physical exhaustion. Still, he had strength enough left to carry her over to a shady corner where under an old beech-tree stood a rustic seat.

He set Elsie down in this secluded spot, knelt beside her, and putting his arms about her buried his face in her downy bosom feeling like a Buddhist who had at last attained Nirvana.

And, no doubt, he had at that particular moment. For Nirvana is to the Buddhist what home is to the wanderer. And what is home but mankind's first and last pillow—a woman's breast—and a pair of loving arms?

It must have been nearly a quarter of an hour later, when, at last, John lifted his head from its resting-place, and gazed long into Elsie's deep beautiful eyes which seemed indeed to be the "windows of her soul."

"Can you ever forgive me Elsie?"

"For what?" she murmured.

"For letting myself go like this?"

"I would never have forgiven you if you hadn't."

"But Elsie darling . . ."

"What?"

"Do you really, really love me?"

"Of course I do; didn't you know that long ago?"

"How could I?"

"You could have asked me if I did, for instance."

"I never dared."

"Why?"

"I was too terrified of losing your friendship." Elsie smiled down at him tenderly and said: "You *were* an old silly."

John was too honourable a young fellow to conceal anything from the woman he loved, and so made no secret of the utter hopelessness of his prospects. He told her that beyond his salary from Sir Charles he had not one penny in the world, and not the smallest expectation from anyone: that he would have to depend entirely upon what he could earn to keep a roof over her head, without any particular abilities, capital, or influence, to help him.

Luckily for John, and for romance in general, it is often the way of things that when a woman is a good woman, and when she is in love, it matters nothing to her if the object of her affections happens to be a millionaire, or a tramp in reduced circumstances. So, in spite of everything, John found himself the accepted suitor of no less a person than the stepdaughter of Sir Charles Dorsay, Bart., who was the twelfth successor to the title he bore.

That Elsie's choice of a lover would destroy every prospect of her ever inheriting any portion of the old man's money, both the girl herself and Tarren felt pretty certain. Still, she seemed quite resigned to losing everything.

"What good would all that money be?" she had said earnestly, "if I were to lose you? Whatever *you* are able to give me I'll love for the sake of the giver. But however little it is I'll love it just the same. You know, John dear, some girls think of getting married just as if it were getting some kind of job on 'live-in and all found' terms, and they get wild if their husbands can't give them everything they need. Now I think it's something quite different. It's just when a man and a woman live together always because they'd both fret to death if they didn't."

And John Tarren had silently thanked God for the greatest of all life's gifts—the love of a good woman.

CHAPTER II

IT WAS NOT THE PROBABILITY of disinheritance, but her fear of her lover being dismissed, and so separated from her, that made Elsie insist that John should say nothing to Sir Charles Dorsay about their relationship. After some little hesitation he agreed, and the pair cherished their sweet secret in their breasts without the baronet appearing so much as to suspect that they were anything more than friends.

Meanwhile, of course, John was making continual efforts to find himself another post; and, better to qualify himself for a really good position, was taking a correspondence course in accountancy.

Elsie was nearing her twenty-first birthday, and he hoped, by making every possible effort, he might be able to leave the service of Sir Charles shortly after his step-daughter attained her majority, and to have a home to offer her in about a year's time.

Both hoped that it could be managed much sooner, for, altogether apart from their longing for each other and a little home of their own, they both loathed every moment of their association with Sir Charles Dorsay.

And well they might, for there never was such a disagreeable, self-centred autocrat. He was tall, thin, sinister-looking, and grey-haired: a hooknosed, haughty tyrant: the kind of man who is only happy when surrounded by dependants whom he could lash with his sarcastic tongue to his heart's content, and who dare not retaliate for fear of being driven from the house to swell the ranks of the unemployed with no reference, and, consequently, little hope of finding another situation. And, moreover, Dorsay was careful in selecting his servants to engage only those whose circumstances made the prospect of being jobless too terrible to contemplate.

He knew that poor John Tarren was no exception to the general rule, and so made his secretary's life a burden to him in every way he could.

And what a time John had of it to be sure: for apart from Dorsay's bad temper, and the disagreeable sneering patronage he inflicted on all those around him, there were other traits in his character which made him no credit to the title he bore.

For one thing he indulged in periodical bouts of heavy drinking, during which he would pick quarrels innumerable about nothing at all, and end up by chasing "violet lobsters" and "pink rats" out of the library with a loaded gun—a proceeding dangerous enough to everyone; but especially so to John, since Sir Charles would insist that he had personally introduced this alcoholic vermin into the house with the express object of annoying his employer.

If this had been all there was to put up with, Elsie and John would not have minded so much—unpleasant as it was. But it was not, for, when they had been lovers for about two months, Sir Charles, all of a sudden, began to take a noticeable interest in his step-daughter.

He started, of course, by realising one day that "little Elsie had grown up." Next he made the discovery that she was "a damned pretty girl," and expressed the opinion that she "must be made a great fuss of."

From that moment he lavished every expensive present on her, and the "good-night" and "good-morning" kisses—which, of course, dated from Elsie's childhood and had never been stopped by either party—developed from the most casual of forehead-pecks to a species of twice-daily struggle, conducted, on Sir Charles' part, in a way that made Tarren long to kick him.

Sir Charles Dorsay had taken an interest in a good few women in his day, and none of them had come to any particular good, and Eisie very quickly realised what this change in her stepfather's attitude meant, and implored her lover to take her away with all possible speed. He, of course, promised to do so, and, in the meantime, to protect her from her persecutor in so far as lay in his power.

This was no easy matter: for, in addition to the fact that John looked to Dorsay for every penny he had in the world, the old fellow was careful to see that his secretary was well out of earshot before pestering Elsie with his "love-making" which objectionable favour, by the way, was couched in vaguely suggestive hints when the sixty-year-old Romeo happened to be sober—a very rare happening indeed—and took the less delicate form of open insult spoken in a dialect Elsie was too innocent to understand when he was not being, at all times, accompanied by much attempted mauling of her person by "crawley-paws" having a lifetime of experience.

When this sort of thing had gone on for about a fortnight, and Sir Charles found that his stepdaughter would not countenance his advances, he suddenly changed his tactics; and, managing to get Elsie to "give him a few minutes in the library," one fine evening, then and there asked her to marry him.

Elsie, of course, refused point-blank. For, apart from the fact that she had disposed of herself elsewhere, and her loathing of the very sight of Sir Charles, such a marriage would not have been legal.

She used this last objection as the main excuse for her refusal.

Naturally enough there was a fearful scene. But, instead of being furiously angry, as she had feared, he became maudlin, and slobbered over her, grovelling at her feet: and, misquoting odd verses from the Scriptures, relating to the marriage-tie, threatened to shoot himself if she would not relent.

Elsie, who could stand it no longer, rushed away to her room where she locked herself in, fearful that the old man would follow her or carry out his threat of self-destruction on the spot. But the worst did not happen. Left alone, Sir Charles babbled to the empty chair for a few minutes, and then dropped off into a drunken sleep. Half an hour later Tarren and the butler got him into bed—and Elsie breathed freely again.

The following morning Dorsay apologised to his stepdaughter for having upset her the previous night by being "not quite himself," and again "popped the question." This time, however, there was an important sequel. Sir Charles produced from his desk sundry legal documents the contents of which he expounded to Elsie; who found, to her annoyance, that she was not the stepdaughter of the man before her, but only his ward.

She had been the adopted daughter of the woman she had always imagined to be her real mother, and to whom Sir Charles had been the second husband.

So her trump card—the relationship—was gone. But, nevertheless, she braced herself up, and told Sir Charles finally that there never could be any question of marriage between them, and that this was her final word on the subject.

Dorsay took this now painfully personal refusal wonderfully quietly. He just said he was sadly disappointed, and hinted—in a voice betraying, perhaps, just a trace of hidden snarl—that it was "better to be an old man's darling than a young man's slave."

Elsie wondered if he could possibly know about John and trembled. But, although things after this interview were strained, Dorsay pestered her no more, although he followed her about on slippered feet wherever she went.

Again she wondered if he knew of her affair with Tarren. It was certainly a fact that from now on he treated his secretary even worse than he had before, inflicting every possible petty humiliation upon him that lay in his power. Especially did he take a delight in taunting John with his poverty and dependence in the presence of the servants, as well as in the presence of Elsie herself.

Tarren just got on with his work and said nothing, and the lovers still refrained from any mention of their engagement in case Dorsay merely suspected and nothing more. They decided it was better to "let sleeping dogs lie" and wait quietly until Elsie should have attained her majority and John had another, and better, job.

Then they would elope and live happily ever after.

For full three weeks after Elsie had refused to marry him Sir Charles did not go away from home as was his wont, and the lovers had a dreadful time of it, listening for those slippered feet during the few secret meetings that they could snatch together.

If only Dorsay would take one of his trips to London or go off to Paris for a week-end as he used to.

One fine day, however, towards the end of August, it seemed that their wish was to be granted, for, after breakfast, Sir Charles announced his intention of going to London, and not returning until the following morning.

The lovers were overjoyed at the idea of twenty-four hours' liberty. Their happiness, however, was somewhat dispelled by the tyrant all but throwing a bundle of unanswered correspondence at his secretary with instructions to "answer them all without fail by this evening's post!"

So poor John had to rattle away on the typewriter the whole of the golden August day, while the disconsolate Elsie tried to console herself with a book, the comfort of a hammock in the really beautiful old-world garden of "Dorsay Hall," and a box of chocolates which her lover had secretly provided her with the night before.

Truly they met at lunch and at tea-time; but Corbin, the butler, hovered about throughout both meals. Elsie hardly dare tell him to leave the room for fear of the information going back to the absent monster; and, indeed, it did seem as if the man had been told to spy upon them. His little ferret's eyes gleamed at her whenever she was not looking at him, and the lovers took warning.

But that evening was Corbin's evening out, and Elsie and John hoped that they might be able to snatch an hour or so together when he was gone.

And he was not due back until midnight.

At last the final letter was written and addressed. Tarren pushed his machine aside, and, tearing a sheet of postage-stamps into strips, commenced a quick-fire stamping of the envelopes. This done he rang the bell, glancing again at the clock as he did so.

It was nearly eight.

In answer to his ring the butler knocked at the door and was told to "come in." He was a tall, dark-haired, upright man, sallow skinned, and sinister-looking, with eyes which, as mentioned before, were set close together, and gleamed unpleasantly.

Tarren handed him the mail to post, and, remarking that the day had gone very quickly, brought up the point that the clock was on the verge of striking eight, and so Corbin need not bother about returning to "Dorsay Hall" until midnight when his leave terminated.

It was so carefully suggested that, in spite of the fact that he had actually been instructed by Sir Charles to watch Tarren the whole day, the butler did not see the motive for John giving him an extra half-hour off. Instead he felt a little pleased at being released early, and, with his eternal "Very Good Sir," took the letters and left the room.

As soon as the door had closed behind Corbin, John rose to his feet with a yawn and stretched himself, just as the clock from the hall boomed out eight. He covered up the typewriter and locked the drawers of his desk, after which he glanced across the library at Sir Charles' big writing table which was conspicuous in the centre just as if to make sure the baronet was not sitting there, heaved a great sigh of relief at his heavy day's work being finished, and walked out of the oak panelled apartment into the slightly more cheerful diningroom.

Finding this quite deserted, he made his way to the lounge, where, to his joy, he came across the object of his search. Elsie was seated on a large couch drawn up an-glewise in front of the old fireplace, deep in a copy of *The Graphic.* She did not hear her lover enter, and, realising this, he crept up behind her and gently passed both his hands in front of her eyes.

With a little scream Elsie sprang to her feet, and a few seconds later she was in his arms.

"Why, John darling, how you startled me! Have you finished all those dreadful letters?"

"Just finished dearest. Corbin's gone with them to the post. I told him he need not bother to come back. So the old spy is out of the way till midnight."

"Thank Heaven!"

"Thank Heaven indeed. Did you see him looking at us during lunch and tea? I feel sure Sir Charles set him on to watch us."

"Shouldn't be at all surprised if he did. It would be just like him. Sometimes I almost feel frightened of him. He hangs round me like some horrible evil spirit. I never feel safe."

"Surely the old fellow hasn't been pestering you any more!"

"Oh, not exactly pestering me, John dear: that's to say he has not been doing any more love-making. But he seems always creeping about, eyeing me like a beast of prey. I never quite realised how I loathed the sight of him until to-day. The place is quite nice without him, and I've had quite a happy day of it."

"Elsie! And while I've not been able to get a sight of you!"

"You dear old silly, you know I don't mean that at all. I've thought of nothing but you all day; if only you had been with me it would have been a day of utter Paradise. There now!"

"And now I *am* here . . ."

"Now my happiness is perfect . . . or at least . . ."

"At least . . .?" he queried.

"Well, at least, it would be if we were not in this gloomy old mansion, under the thumb of that terrible old man, but in our own place and . . ."

"Married and done for," he finished.

She laughed and blushed.

"Something very like it," she smiled. Then, suddenly, she became serious. "Oh, John dear: how on earth are we going to live through the next few days? Thank God I'll be out of all this when I am of age!"

"Yes, you'll be able to get out of it all in a very little while now, Elsie," replied Tarren, "but God knows how long I shall have to stick here treated worse than a dog by a man not fit to own one, and longing, all the while, to be able to make a home for you when I could not so much as support myself outside this wretched place. I've tried and tried— written letters and answered advertisements till it's nearly driven me crazy, but I simply can't so much as get an answer. There seems to be as much competition for a clerical job carrying a few hundreds a year as there is for the Prime Ministership at election-time. God knows by what fluke I managed to get taken on here. I suppose because nobody else would tolerate Sir Charles for five minutes."

"You poor, silly old thing, don't you know you got this job for no other reason than because you were the best of the bunch, and, if it were not for things being so dreadful in the country, you wouldn't have the least little bit of trouble in finding a perfectly marvellous job anywhere. But things will pick up, never fear, and you'll get a splendid post. Just keep on trying and don't worry."

She put her arms round his neck and kissed him, set his tie to rights, and led him to the couch.

"Now come and sit beside me and cheer up like a good boy. Everything is going to be wonderful after all."

John allowed himself to be sat down, but his brow was, none the less, troubled. She noticed this, and sat upon his knee with a flop, opened her bag which lay on the settee nearby, and, taking therefrom a carmine lipstick container, playfully traced the wrinkles on his face with the sharpened end, afterwards holding up the tiny mirror in the flap before her lover's face that he might admire her work of art.

"There now. Just look at those wrinkles! You look as if you were a hundred."

"I feel a thousand."

"Poor old fellow. Oh, look; another great deep furrow over your eyebrow. Take about sixpenny-worth of lipstick to fill that one in."

John couldn't help smiling at the way she recommenced tracing his wrinkles, and his face certainly did look rather funny in the miniature looking-glass held up for his inspection. He laughed in spite of himself.

"It's all very well for you, Elsie, to be so cheerful. I suppose you have got an aunt or somewhere you can go to when you come of age, and only a few days to wait. But what about me—got to stick here until I can get another job. And I was two years getting this one. And what a one it is."

"John! And if you hadn't got it you would never have known about me. How can you?"

Tarren kissed her upturned face.

"My darling, I know. And because it brought you into my life I bless it with my whole heart. There! But now I have met you, I don't know what on earth to do about it. I've got absolutely nothing in the world to offer you. I'm just a beggar—as Sir Charles has been careful to point out to you, no doubt."

Elsie kissed him fondly.

"You've given me the biggest thing in the world, John. All that matters to me."

"And that?"

"You."

"All very well, dearest, but we can't live on love, you know."

There was a slightly troubled silence. Then Elsie began to speak slowly and thoughtfully. "John dear."

"Yes darling, what is it?"

"You do really, really, love me, don't you?"

"Yes sweetheart, more than all the world. That's what makes me so worried about things. I couldn't bear to think of my having inflicted any poverty on you by taking you away from all this."

"And you really don't mind a bit even if old Sir Charles does cut me off with a penny when I tell him I'm going to marry you in spite of everything, the very minute we can get as much as a bed-sitting-room? He won't let me have a single halfpenny, you know. Not that I want his old money."

"My darling, it troubles me that your love for me should cost you so much. But, for myself, I want just you— sometimes I almost wish you had been just a poor little servant girl instead of what you are: although, then, perhaps, I should never have known how much you love me!"

"And you wouldn't mind marrying a poor little beggar?"

"No indeed beloved. I want you at all costs. But—Oh God; to find a home to put you in and enough to give you to eat. It's driving me mad."

Elsie put her arms round his neck. "Don't worry, John dearest: it can't be helped a bit. Let's forget all our worries, dear, just for to-night. He'll be back again to-morrow; and, till then, let's just think of each other and dream of the future till Corbin gets back and starts spying again."

"You're sure Sir Charles won't come back to-night—just to catch us on the hop?"

"Quite certain darling. I heard him telling Corbin to put his night-clothes in his bag. Depend upon it he's seeing green rats by now, and consoling himself with some barmaid in London. He'll be pretty late to-morrow, too, and have such a head he'll drive us all crazy."

"I hope you're right, sweetheart. It would be awful if he were to find us together here."

"Don't let's even think of it: it gives me cold shivers down my spine. He'd turn me out of the house in jealous rage, and give you the sack! It would be too awful. But still I'm sure we're as safe as houses to-night."

"What about Corbin? Suppose he came back extra early just to spy. He'd be sure to tell Sir Charles."

"I'm quite sure he wouldn't. I took the precaution of giving him a pound as he went out. And, besides, he's taken the housemaid to the theatre 'cause I saw the tickets. And, if he should come in early, he'll not be sober. He's as bad as old

Sir Charles that way. He'd only think he was seeing things again."

Reassured, John heaved a sigh of relief, and the lovers settled themselves down in the comfort of the settee to snatch an evening of happiness together. By this time the shadows had fallen and it was practically dark. Tarren reached out his hand for the switch of a reading-lamp on a nearby table, but Elsie stopped him.

"Don't let's put on any light. Put on the electric fire instead: it'll make a lovely cosy glow, and it's quite shivery tonight, anyway."

Tarren did as he was desired, and the polished copper electric bowl fire standing in the old-world hearth sizzled into a deep red orb of light—like a glowing, crimson, sunset. It threw a warm and comfortably dim radiance across the tiger-skin on to the leather couch, enabling the lovers just to see each other's faces, and leaving the rest of the room in deep shadow.

"Now let's be happy," murmured Elsie, cuddling herself on her sweetheart's knee with her arms about him.

It was not many moments before they were nestled together on the great settee like the two love-birds they were. A little faintly murmured conversation: then, as if words were no longer necessary, there fell a silence.

The evening was perfectly still, the quiet being only made more intense by the solemn ticking of the Grandfather clock in the background, and the very occasional rumble of a distant car as it passed by the old Manor House. Snuggled together in comfort on the great downy couch the lovers soon forgot their troubles in the rapture of each other's arms, content to let the world go by unheeded.

Bathed in the warm glow of the electric "sun," and the still warmer glow of mutual love, each dreamily at peace because of the clinging nearness of the other; it was, perhaps not altogether surprising that, as the time wore on towards midnight, they became more and more sleepy—particularly as neither had passed very good nights of late—worried as they both were at the state of things. Tarren, too, had done a

hard day's work. So it was not long before his quiet breathing told Elsie that he had fallen asleep. His cheek was pil-
lowed on the top of her head which nestled against his
shoulder. She murmured drowsily, clasped him just a little
tighter; and, after a very little while indeed, was in the land
of dreams too.

It was long before John and Elsie were conscious of anything
beyond a dreamy satisfaction at the clinging warmth of each
other. Once or twice the girl stirred and murmured in her
sleep only to settle down again in a new position in her
lover's arms. And even when they did become slightly conscious of their surroundings they were both, to all intents and
purposes, fast asleep.

Elsie's first impression was the muffled booming of the
clock striking. She counted the chimes in her dreams. Eleven
o'clock: they must wake up soon—Corbin would be back in
an hour and they must get to bed before he could find them
there: still—perhaps it was only a dream clock that struck—
or perhaps . . . Oh! well, in any case there was an hour: she
must keep awake—or rather not sleep any more heavily—
and listen out for the quarter-hour to strike—or would it be
time enough when the half-hour struck? Yes there would . . .
"poor John is so tired," she mused . . . "so . . . VERY . . .
tired . . ."

She was fast asleep again.

The next thing Elsie knew was that she was dreaming that
she and John had fallen asleep in each other's arms, and that
somebody was watching them and laughing at them . . . horribly . . . It was too bad of Corbin . . . especially after she had
given him that pound . . . and . . . Oh! . . . of course . . . it is a
dream . . . He's not back yet . . . he couldn't be . . . the quarter hadn't struck yet . . . no . . . it's just striking now . . .

The clock did strike: the quarter: the half: the three quarter.

Heavens! She must have dropped off to sleep again.

The Hour!!! Good Lord! It must be midnight . . . Listen . . .

The clock began to boom out . . . Elsie strained her ears to catch the strokes. Clear and ominous came the sound through the girl's sleep-drugged brain . . .

One.

Dead silence.

A second later Elsie had opened her eyes wildly and sprang to her feet. Her sudden movement woke up Tarren who blinked dazedly at her for a second or two.

Then he, too, jumped from the couch—sharing with her that terrible, utterly futile, realisation which always breaks upon one after having slept through a critical moment.

Great God. It was one o'clock in the morning: Corbin must be back: someone, too, had turned on the standard electric lamp: the door was gaping wide open: a cold draught was blowing in upon them from the hall outside.

And there, standing facing them, one elbow resting upon the mantelshelf: a half-sodden cigar hanging from his mouth, and an awful glare in his bloodshot eyes, was *Sir Charles Dorsay.*

CHAPTER III

IF ELSIE AND JOHN thought that this sudden and unexpected return of Sir Charles, after his announced intention of being away until the morning, was nothing more or less than a trap set for the express purpose of tripping them up, they were not very far from the truth.

Ever since Elsie's point-blank refusal of his heart and hand, the baronet had his suspicions of John Tarren's being his master's rival. He had watched the couple very carefully from the first moment of the birth of this idea, but could find nothing to confirm it—so successful had the lovers been in keeping their secret to themselves. Failing to get evidence in this way—which evidence he wanted very badly indeed to set his mind at rest—Dorsay next gave the butler strict instructions to spy upon his secretary and his step-daughter at all times and in all places. The reports made by this worthy were unsatisfactory to a degree: he could be sure of nothing, although he expressed the opinion that "Mr. Tarren was sweet on Miss Elsie." But he could point to no direct proof of this rather vague assertion, and, knowing that much of his very best old brandy went down Corbin's throat whenever his back happened to be turned, and, at the same time, having personal experience of the effects on the eyesight of such potations, Dorsay rather discounted the oft-repeated assertion by his butler that "Mr. Tarren didn't 'alf wink at Miss Elsie whenever he got the chance."

A week or so later the butler brought his master something in the nature of concrete evidence. It was a snapshot taken with a five shilling camera, and rather badly developed at that. It depicted the summer-house interior; and showed, tolerably clearly, two white-clad figures therein sitting together with arms round one another's neck and cheek against cheek.

But so bad had, evidently, been the light when the snap was taken that it was impossible to identify so much as the summer-house—let alone the two figures inside. Even the professional enlargement of the photograph to some twenty times its original size did little more than confirm the fact that the figures were, respectively, those of a man and a woman.

Still, it brought out the summer-house sufficiently clearly for identification as something so like that at "Dorsay Hall" to warrant the matter being investigated further.

So Sir Charles, after his first violent fit of jealous fury had abated, decided to take the matter in hand. A few days later, therefore, he announced his avowed intention, as we already know, of going to London and spending the night there.

He was, actually, going to do nothing of the kind. He was going to pay a quite local visit instead. And, truth to tell, that visit was somewhat pressingly necessary.

And this is how that was:—Sir Charles Dorsay, in common with quite a few other men of means and leisure—to say nothing of a miniature army of others of the same habits though of little leisure and no means at all—had a considerable number of lady friends of a kind that could hardly be invited to "Dorsay Hall"; and, in consequence, had to be entertained as great a distance away from home as was possible. Being a moderate man he seldom had more than one of these charmers in favour at a time—since there was, of course, always a considerable female staff at "Dorsay Hall" to fall back upon in case of emergency—and, being a fair one in his dealings, he never permitted any one of them to remain on his good books for too long a period.

This, not unnaturally, led to occasional friction between Sir Charles and one or other of his "beauty-chorus": especially as so warm a friendship as the baronet invariably gave them not infrequently tended to bring about sundry complications, in spite of every known persuasion to the contrary.

Whenever friction of this description occurred, it was generally settled with the assistance of Sir Charles' banker. Money is a wonderful healer of broken hearts and ruined lives—especially when the hearts happen to beat in the friendly breasts of such delicate little morsels as are generally to be found hanging about the West End of London after dark.

Notable exceptions are found, even among such obliging ladies as these. And such a one was Mdlle. Vesta Morone, a Frenchwoman of alleged high descent, who, after being maintained for some six months in a state of great luxury, in a furnished flat in Mayfair, at Sir Charles' personal expense, and for his especial delight, and being told one fine day by no less a person than Dorsay himself to "clear out at once," expressed a rooted objection.

Now, although one can hardly expect it to be believed, it is none the less true that this reluctance to "stand down" in favour of a younger member of her profession on the part of Mdlle. Morone was prompted, not so much by financial considerations, as by a very real affection for the baronet. In point of fact the unhappy woman loved him to distraction in spite of everything, and would have been quite content to have remained his wife in all but law indefinitely, and for no reward other than her little flat, and the joy and honour of her beloved's company on an average of, say, once a week, without the least hope, or even desire, of ever bearing his title, and with no more money than that just necessary to keep herself always young, fresh, and charming, in his eyes.

Had she been rich, or even comfortably off, she would not have wanted even this much payment for the single-minded devotion of a lifetime: and if Dorsay had happened to have been a poor man she would even have gone to the length of turning the tables completely and keeping him—even if it had been by the exercise of her dreadful calling on the streets. And, since, already, we have few illusions about Sir Charles Dorsay, let us at once admit that he would have raised no objection to being so maintained had it been necessary.

It was not however—nor was Mdlle. Morone—and so she found herself in the position of having to look for another "protector" one fine morning just before this story opened. Loving Sir Charles as she did, it may be imagined that the fair lady did not take her dismissal "lying down." So much so that Dorsay found it necessary to have her forcibly ejected by a bailiff, after which he congratulated himself on having closed the matter for good and all.

But Mdlle. Morone was not to be got rid of quite so easily, and so, a few days later, the lady presented herself at one of his London clubs where she managed, by hook or by crook, to get hold of his address.

And so, a few days later, to his very great annoyance, Sir Charles Dorsay discovered that his cast-off light-o'-love knew where he lived, and had actually installed herself in a nearby Commercial Hotel. Several times she presented herself at "Dorsay Hall" and demanded to see the master of the house; only, of course, to be informed by Corbin that "Sir Charles was away from home."

So she tried other tactics. Finding that the butler was quite incorruptible—at least by a purse so shallow as hers—she wrote a letter to her beloved imploring him to see her, either at "Dorsay Hall" or outside it. Getting no reply to several such epistles—in more than one of which she threatened to commit suicide—she came to the very natural conclusion that if one wants to force anyone to do any particular thing through fear, it must always be through the fear of what might happen to *them* if they refused; and *not* what might befall anyone else.

The consequence was she wrote yet another letter demanding that Sir Charles should meet her at a certain hotel some miles or so away that very evening, and saying that, if he failed to do so, she should go straight to the local paper and tell them the whole story. Not only so, but she threatened further that when, in due course, she became a happy mother she would furnish true particulars as to the parentage of the child when she registered it, and sue the father for maintenance.

Now Sir Charles had not exactly a good name in the district already, although local scandal had not got hold of anything more concrete than vague servants' gossip as yet. Further as very little happened in the village the local rag would, naturally, be delighted to publish anything that smacked of sensation. So Sir Charles determined that he would keep the appointment even if it cost him another hundred pounds or two.

Not only so, but he saw in this sudden summons a chance of "killing two birds with one stone." He could settle in his own mind once and for all his suspicions regarding Elsie and Tarren. John was far too cheap and valuable a servant to sack on a charge which might be no more than a figment of a jealous mind. So Sir Charles gave out that he was going to London and would not be back until the following morning. As the evening he absented himself happened also to be Corbin's evening out, he knew that this would give the lovers—if lovers they were—the chance they wanted to snatch a few hours to themselves. He arranged for Corbin to drive straight to the hotel where he expected to interview the heartbroken Mdlle. Morone, and inform him that Elsie and John were all but alone in the house. He would then motor straight back to "Dorsay Hall" and—as he expected to arrive in about an hour from his time of starting out—he thought it quite possible that he would interrupt a very pretty little love-scene, his victims having plenty of time in which to set the stage.

He found Mdlle. Morone in anything but a charming mood. She wept, raved, and swore; begged, prayed, and beseeched, in a hysterical jumble of French and English, that he should "take her back." Dorsay did all he could to temporise with her: said he would "certainly think seriously about the matter": that he would "see that she was well provided for": and so forth. But Vesta did not want "provisions to be made," she wanted Sir Charles himself, and told him so with many bitter tears.

"That's all very well, me dear," said he, in answer to her frenzied implorations: "but, you see, I just don't happen to want you any longer."

"Ah, I know . . . you want other women . . . women younger and more beautiful than I: women who want you only for the money you bring them: women who, when you are gone, will laugh at your memory from the arms of younger men to whom they have given their hearts. But I— I—*love* you Charlie, and I have loved no other as I love you, and, if you will listen to me, I will remain faithful till death for nothing more than to see you sometimes—to look at you—and for you to try to love me too just a little now and then."

"Sorry, but it can't be done."

"Ah you say that just to tease me. Can you really not want me? I who love you so that, even if you should strike me to your feet, I would kiss the dear hand that did hurt me so . . . and like it that you did hit me!"

Dorsay laughed coldly and lighted a cigar. "Very nice of you I'm sure, Vesta, but really I have no further use for you. Come now, don't complain. I have already given you three hundred pounds, and to-night I offer you another five hundred. Take the cheque and leave me in peace."

But the woman still clung to him sobbing and imploring, trying to kiss and caress him. He shook her off violently.

"Don't maul me about, woman! Stop it I tell you! I'm sick of you and your kind. Sick to death. I want no more of you damned harlots. I'm going to be married again—and to a decent woman."

Somewhat to his surprise, Vesta became a little calmer.

"So?" said she, "you think I don't know all about that too? You are very foolish Charlie not to know it is stupid for a man like you to want what they call a 'good' woman. These 'good' women what are they but 'bad' ones of the most expensive kind that do make you give them everything you have in the whole world, and bind yourself to them for life in front of two witnesses, before they will let you have what you want."

Dorsay laughed in spite of himself as he retorted: "Well, the one I have in mind is worth it anyway."

"You think that because she is new and young. How about when you are tired of her, and not able to go away from her not for one little minute, hein?—when she will go with you everywhere, except when you go to the bathroom—and then she wait outside the door? how about that Charlie?"

"You have had my answer."

But Vesta continued to plead. "Take me back," she begged. "I will not worry you like a wife—just as long as you are by my side sometimes when you are tired of everything else, Charlie, that is all I want. Why will you give me nothing because I love you so, and the other woman everything you have in the world when she do not like you at all—only your money? Listen, Charlie, she will not understand you as I do. She will say that you are bad because you like being bad, while I, who am bad also, will know that you are only bad because you are made like that. It is only one like I that could love you. This good woman could not, and, if you marry her, you will find that 'East is East'."

Dorsay shrugged his shoulders. "If you talk all night," said he, "it will make no difference. I've done with you for good and all. If you pester me further I'll put the police on you and risk any scandal. That's my last word. Now, there's your cheque, take it. What you do with it is your business. I'm off. We shall never meet again."

The woman turned and faced him. "You make a great mistake," said she, in a voice trembling with passion, "we *will* meet again. You are a young man no longer, Charlie, and the time is near when you will be called away. And what then? Perhaps it will be that you feel no more and know no more for ever. But, perhaps, it will be that you go to another world; and, if so, what will you find there to comfort you? Your dead wife was what you call a 'good' woman: like, also, no doubt, your mother. So they will not know you there since you also are not good. They will be too occupied with great things of the spirit world even to realize you are near them. So you will be alone Charlie—so alone that your heart will break—and you will know that you are in hell. And it is there you will find my arms waiting for you: for, even if le bon Dieu say that I suffer so in this world that I may go to heaven in the next, good or bad, I will climb right down into hell if it is there I find you. And you will come to me Charlie: come thankfully to the love of the poor lost woman, which will be the only love that can reach you there, because like that of the dog, it cares not if the thing it loves be good or bad."

Vesta had barely finished speaking when there suddenly came an impatient banging at the door. Dorsay, who had been a little bewildered at the passionate outburst of Mdlle. Morone, thankful for an interruption, opened the door at once.

Corbin stood breathless on the threshold.

"Quick Guv'nor," he panted, "they're at it."

With a snarl of fury, Dorsay seized his hat and stick, and turned to go without so much as another look at Vesta. She rushed at him trying to follow him, or, at least, get in another word before he left. With a violent oath he flung her from him with so much force that she fell headlong to the ground, narrowly escaping striking her head on the fender.

Before she could struggle to her feet the door had banged, and the whirr of a powerful car broke the stillness of the night.

She dashed out of the room and downstairs to the street. But only a red spot fast vanishing in the direction of "Dorsay Hall"—the rear light of Sir Charles' car—was visible in the darkness.

For a few seconds she stood like a statue looking after the vanishing Rolls. Her face was white with fury, and her eyes burned with concentrated passion.

"Nom de Dieu!" she hissed between her clenched teeth, "perhaps you will be called away . . . sooner than you think!"

CHAPTER IV

PERHAPS ONE THING before all others has made the English-
man master of half the world—he never loses his head in a
crisis. And so when John Tarren saw who it was standing
there watching him, instead of collapsing like a "guilty one
accused," he pulled himself together in less than a second,
smoothed his ruffled hair, arranged his tie and, taking his
cigarette-case from his pocket, lighted up, blowing a great
cloud of smoke across the lounge as he faced his furious employer.

"Hello, sir," he said casually, "you're back early."

As to Elsie, she stood swaying slightly and holding on to
the edge of the settee. It seemed to her that the room was
spinning round. Tarren gently slipped his arm round her and
sat her down in the corner of the couch farthest away from
Dorsay. She lay back feeling faint and dizzy, thankful that
her lover seemed to be able to grapple with the situation, and
wondering dazedly exactly what was going to happen.

"I'm not sorry you changed your mind about spending the
night in Town," went on John coolly, "I've wanted a few
words with you very badly for some time past. And here's an
opportunity ready-made."

Sir Charles was utterly taken aback. He had expected anything but this. He chewed violently at what remained of his
cigar, got a stray strip of tobacco-leaf in the back of his
throat, coughed, swore, and finally spat the wet stump right
into his secretary's face, together with a generous ration of
saliva mixed with nicotine and stale brandy.

His face was black with rage. It was only with difficulty
he could find words.

"You slimy skunk!" he hissed: "so that's the way you go
on when your master's back is turned is it? Interfere with his

ward do you? By God, it's a good thing I was not away all
night. Otherwise . . ."

But John broke in quickly, "Look here, sir, if you are going to conduct this . . . er . . . this interview . . . like a Spanish
circus proprietor, instead of an English gentleman, don't you
think we'd better send Miss Mervyn to her room before we
begin?"

Here Elsie suddenly seemed to get a grip upon her facul-
ties once more and broke in sharply, "No, John, I'm not going to be sent away. I'm going to stay here and see this
through with you."

"Yes, you shall stay here all right," roared Sir Charles.
"I'd just like your boy friend to get what's coming to him in
front of his lady-love."

With these words Sir Charles turned half round and
shouted into the hall—"Corbin!"

"Here sir," and the butler entered the lounge still in his
overcoat.

"Ring for all the other servants will you! I've caught this
dog very nearly in the act, and I want to let the female staff
see what happens to people who interfere with women under
my care."

Corbin saw his chance to toady and took it. "Very good,
sir . . . very good, sir," he smiled; "certainly, sir . . . certainly
. . . but . . . if I might presume so far, sir . . , forgive the liberty . . . but both the maids are . . , hem . . . *undressed,* sir . . .
and in bed . . . and for me to go to their rooms alone . . . at
this hour sir . . . well . . . *I* would not exactly care to suggest . . . any undue intimacy sir—even with women of my
own station."

He broke off smiling and rubbing his hands, hoping that
Sir Charles had seen the point. Sir Charles had, and was delighted. "Quite right, Corbin," he said shortly: "but I should
like you to stay. Sorry to drag you into such a nasty business,
but, if all my *servants* were as scrupulous as you are, it
would not be necessary."

Dorsay was not the only one present who saw through
Corbin's remarks. Elsie flushed crimson, and shot the man a

look that made him shrink with the nearest approach to shame he had ever experienced.

"You swine!" she said in a low voice.

At Sir Charles' reply however she sprang to her feet in righteous indignation.

"How dare you say such things—how dare you insinuate that John and I . . .," she began. But Sir Charles laughed, and looked at her in a way that made her feel sick.

Tarren interposed.

"Sit down Elsie—please," said he, "just let me handle this: that hound of a butler is not worth noticing anyway." Then turning to Sir Charles, he said:—"If you have anything to say to me I should think you have the common decency to say it in private. You must know, perfectly well, that you have no right to bring your butler into this. If you are really worthy of the title you bear you will send Corbin away."

"And who the flaming hell do you think you're talking to?" bellowed the infuriated owner of "Dorsay Hall," with a horrible oath: "and what in God's name do you think you are? I'll tell you one thing about yourself that you ought to have realised long ago—you're my hireling, my servant— just as Mr. Corbin is. There is only one difference between you. He knows his rank and behaves himself, and you don't."

Both John and Elsie noticed the "Mr." tacked on to the butler's name and its implication: also that the man's head seemed to swell visibly at hearing himself thus spoken of to a man whom he had, not so very long ago, addressed as "Sir."

With an effort Tarren kept his temper. "This is beside the point," he retorted, "let us get down to things that matter. I am not in the least ashamed of being surprised here alone with Elsie. As I said I have long wanted a word with you about her. I don't mind much how you take it, but she has done me the very great honour of agreeing to become my wife."

"Yes I have," added Elsie, "and it's no use your trying to do anything about it. I shall be of age in a few days and can please myself—and it's a shame of you trying to treat John as if he were a servant. You must know that he is your equal in birth and education as well as I do."

"Thank you, Elsie," put in John, and then to Sir Charles:—"So, sir, I have the pleasure of asking you for the hand of your ward."

Instead of breaking out afresh in savage rage as both Elsie and John thought he would, Dorsay laughed, after hearing them both through in silence.

"Listen to stainless honour!" he sneered. "He says he's going to marry her! Didn't his mother educate him beautifully? So it's gone as far as that, has it, by your own showing?" he added to John, in a tone of voice that made the latter long to knock him down. "Well, well, well. What *are* we going to do? If it were one of the female servants you'd got entangled with, we might let it all have a happy ending. But as it is—" and his voice became menacing with a snarl impossible to describe—"we can only give you the thrashing you deserve and hope that your sweetie'll keep it dark for her own sake, and that Dr. Barnar . . ."

"Shut up," shouted John, whose blood was now thoroughly up. Had Dorsay been a young man he would, most unquestionably, have measured his length on the floor at that very moment. "What sort of man are you to make such filthy insinuations about your own ward? How dare you make such suggestions about either of us! I tell you that there is not the remotest basis of truth in what you are hinting at: nor do I believe, for one moment, that you seriously think that there is. Still, your words are, none the less, a foul insult, and, if you think I am going to stand here and listen to your vile slander of the woman who is to become my wife, you are damned well mistaken!"

"He thinks I'm mistaken, Corbin!"—jeered the baronet—"mistaken! . . . By God! . . . at my age, and about a puppy like he is! Listen to me, you impudent scoundrel!" he shouted at John:—"you don't suppose, do you, that I imagine that Miss Elsie would debase herself with a cur like you, picked out of the London gutter with a newspaper? Of course not. You damned fool! Don't you know she was only having a game with you to pass away an idle hour? She wouldn't let you touch her fingertips however you might try. It's your blasted impertinence at daring to look at her you're going to be kicked for!"

Elsie was on her feet in an instant. "Stop"—she called out to Dorsay—"please understand that I *do* love John—and it is my intention to marry him too!"

"Not really," leered Sir Charles.

"Yes, really," replied Elsie, "and ever since we met he has behaved as the most chivalrous of gentlemen. His attitude to me has been spotless—which is more than yours has!" she added, with a flash of anger.

Dorsay laughed again. "Has it indeed. Well, I'll take your word for that my dear. But that makes his damned cheek none the less. No doubt the young fellow is smart enough to see that he can't treat you as he would one of his own class—or perhaps what he wants from you is something a little different from what the girls in his native alley were diddled into giving him, before he wormed his way into decent society. Oh yes, it's quite possible that he has been playing Sir Galahad with you. It always impresses a romantic young woman—and it pays when she is heiress to a quarter of a million while the stainless knight is a pennyless vagabond."

"How dare you say such things!" said Elsie brokenly, the tears running down her cheeks, "John loves me from his heart, and you are a wicked old beast even to suggest that he doesn't."

"Don't be a fool, girl," replied Dorsay. "It's your prospects he's after. He knows I've got about a quarter of a million and this estate, and that you are my heiress: he knows, too, that you are young and inexperienced and I am old and one day will hand everything over to you. The puppy wants the money and not you. Why you've said yourself just now that he'd been as cold as ice. Now if he were in love with you . . ."

"How can you be so vile?" sobbed Elsie, crying more with vexation than anything else. "John loves me, I know he does, and love is not what you say it is. You're a horrid, beastly, disgusting old man; and you've treated me shamefully ever since I grew up. You made me hate the sight of you, and think all men were filthy like . . . like you are . . . and now I've met a decent, clean man who loves me . . . you first accuse him of being . . . rotten like you are . . . and then, when he stands up to you, you say he wants me only for the money I'm to have. I don't want your wretched money, I want John, and I *will* have him. Stupid money, you can throw it all in the ditch if you like!"

And Elsie cried as if her heart would break. John was about to put his arms round her when Dorsay, who was watching him narrowly, put out an iron hand and literally threw him out of the way with a violence that made it difficult for him to keep his balance.

"Stand back," he roared, "if ever I catch you tampering with the affections of my ward again, I'll shoot you like the vermin-dog you are! Not that you'll get the chance either. You're sacked—right now, and can clear out of the place at once—when I've done with you."

He turned to where the butler was still standing, "Corbin," he called, "pay this fellow a month's wages in place of a month's notice. I've no cash on me and I wouldn't trust him with a cheque of mine."

Corbin produced a pocket-book, and counted out the notes to the right amount which he handed to Dorsay with a dependant's leer.

Sir Charles pinned them together with a pin from the corner of his coat, and threw the bundle—a very small one needless to say—at John's head. "Take your wages, Tarren," he shouted, "and put them away safely in case they get lost!"

John picked up the money with as much dignity as he could command and put it in his pocket. He was on the point of refusing to accept a penny, but a second's reflection showed him that it would have been folly. Utter destitution faced him.

He bowed stiffly and was about to leave the room, when Elsie suddenly threw her arms round his neck.

"You're not to go," she cried, "you're not to. I won't have it. I love you and I'd go mad without you!"

"But, Elsie dearest, I must," replied Tarren. "Now I'm dismissed I have no right here at all."

"Keep away, damn your soul!" screamed Dorsay as Tarren kissed Elsie good-bye. He seized John by the shoulder and tore him from Elsie's embrace. But the girl clung to her lover so tightly that they nearly toppled over together. Her eyes were blazing and she faced Sir Charles like an angry tigress protecting its young.

"You can sack John if you like!" she said in a voice shaking with emotion, but, none the less, determined:—"and you can keep me here in bondage for a few more days. But at the end of that time I'll be twenty-one and my own mistress. And then I'll leave this horrid old place and go to the man I love—in spite of you!"

"You do," snarled Dorsay, "and I'll not give you a halfpenny—much as I love you. You'll be starving mighty soon with your pauper-knight; and, as you are no relation of mine, I can leave this place—as well as every cent—to charities. And I will too—by the living God—if you dare . . ."

"You can do as you like," blazed Elsie, "we don't care"—then to John—"John, will you swear you don't mind if I haven't a penny in the world. Do you love me—myself?"

John put his arms about her quite fearlessly, and faced Sir Charles squarely, "Yes, I do," he said.

Elsie turned triumphantly to Dorsay. "You hear what he says," said she defiantly—"you hear?"

"I hear him all right," replied Dorsay. "No doubt the lazy hound wants you to keep him. Won't he be lucky too?—you couldn't earn a six pence. Still, perhaps he thinks, since you're a pretty girl, you . . ."

We will not shock the reader by setting down here what Sir Charles said Elsie could do for a living. Let us remark though that he put forth his suggestion in the language of the gutter—which, although, happily for Elsie, was about as understandable to her as Classic Greek would be to a dustman—gave her an uncomfortable feeling that she was being very horribly insulted.

But Tarren understood it, as the baronet knew he would. He flushed a deep crimson, and his fists clenched themselves almost automatically. His eyes blazed with almost uncontrollable rage. But his self-mastery was wonderful. Perhaps he knew that Dorsay was not altogether responsible for what he said at that moment. Nevertheless Tarren gave vent to his feelings in words.

"You filthy beast," he said, in a deep and menacing voice he hardly recognised as his own, "you're not fit to live. If you don't apologise to Elsie I'll kill you . . ."

Tarren's self-control was leaving him fast. He made a stride forward as if he would attack Dorsay. But Elsie intervened.

"Don't, John," she said quickly, "he's not worth it." Then she launched a torrent of words at her guardian.

"John's quite right," said she, "you're not fit to live. And you won't live very long either I hope. I hate you, hate you, hate you, I'm going away from here directly I'm of age—directly. And if you think John and I will starve or that we'll do . . . beastly things for a living . . . either of us . . . you're wrong . . . You don't know that I know it, but my mother left me five thousand pounds in my own right. You only hold it in trust for me till I am of age. After that it's mine. And I have never told John till this moment. So we'll both be all right. But there's one thing I'm sorry I've got the money for, and that is I'd like to starve with John, just to show you how I love him, and I'd like to live with him without even marrying him . . . just to show you I'd rather do that for the man I love and starve into the bargain than marry you, get your title, and all your money, I hate you, hate you, hate you; and I hope you will break your heart with jealousy and rage when John and I are happy together!"

Dorsay turned black in the face as Elsie hurled those impassioned words at him. He had not the least idea she knew that her mother had made separate provision for her. She must have been searching through the papers in his desk and found the copy of the will. It was damnable. Rage, jealousy, and savage hatred of John Tarren, disappointment, thwarted lust, and outraged pride, all battled together in his brain like the beating of a million smiths' hammers. The veins in his forehead stood out like purple cords, and his eyes glowed like live coals. His face was like that of a furious demon. He gasped, and seized hold of the mantelshelf as if in need of support.

For some seconds he opened his mouth, champing his jaws without any sound coming at all. Then, all of a sudden, as if a dam burst, he sprang forward.

"God damn you!" he screamed, and struck the girl full in the face with all his force. She fell to the ground with a shriek. Almost at the same instant John Tarren's hold over himself gave way.

With a furious oath he sprung straight at Dorsay's throat, and the next instant the two men were struggling violently together. In spite of his age John found the old man no easy matter to grapple with; for he had the strength born of fury, and his muscles were hard—possibly from being pickled for years in alcohol. Elsie was quickly on her feet, horrified at the turn things had taken, and trying to induce her lover to stop in case the exertion should give Sir Charles a stroke. Not that she cared much about the old man. It was John himself she was thinking of. She would not have had her lover arrested for manslaughter or worse. And Dorsay was breathing very hard and his eyes protruded horribly already.

Mr. Walter Corbin, as soon as words were succeeded by blows, thought, at once, that he had better make himself scarce. He had a very tender skin and was no hand at boxing. So he crept out of the room at the same minute as Dorsay struck his ward.

And it was some time before he was missed.

In the meantime the tussle went on, first one man seemed to get the upper hand and then the other. Finally, of course, John's youth and recent athletic training told, and he had Dorsay under control.

He would, no doubt, have thrashed the old fellow soundly but for Elsie.

"Do be careful, John dear," she whispered urgently— "he's very old remember. We don't want anything serious to happen to him, do we?"

By this time John had calmed down a little, and he was able to see the force of his sweetheart's reasoning. So, with a parting punch, he sent his late employer tumbling on to the sofa, where he lay panting and exhausted for some seconds, while Elsie stood anxiously by, hoping that he would recover himself without danger of their being involved in any complications.

But Sir Charles was too tough to be upset so easily, although it was quite five minutes before he was sufficiently recovered from the punishment he had received to speak.

When he did recover himself, however, it was to be forced by John to apologise to Elsie for the blow, and for the various insults he had hurled at her that evening. This, somewhat to Tarren's surprise, was comparatively easy to get out of the fellow. In fact the wind seemed almost quite to have been taken out of his sails by the recent struggle with John.

Now that all was quiet Corbin re-appeared like a butterfly coming out after the rain, and asked Sir Charles if there was anything he could do for him.

The answer was merely that he was to see that the whisky decanter in the library was full.

"For," said Dorsay, with a snarl in Elsie's direction, "I am going to spend a couple of hours at my desk there before I go to bed. Going to alter my will," he added with a snarl.

"Very good, sir," smiled the butler, "and shall I show your late secretary out, sir?"

"No, certainly not," broke in Elsie. "Mr. Tarren is not going to-night. He will not leave until tomorrow morning at the very earliest. That's so—isn't it?" This last to Sir Charles.

Dorsay grunted assent, and John and Elsie both shot a glance of triumph at Corbin—who, surprised and not a little disappointed at the turn things had taken, hurried off to fulfill his mission. It was by this time well past three in the morning.

"I shall hand you over to the police in the morning," said Dorsay to Tarren, as he rose to depart for the library. "Brutal thing—fighting a man old enough to be your father. As to you, Elsie Mervyn, I don't admire your taste. If I get my way you'll have an ex-convict for a husband. And you won't like life on five thousand pounds either—you on whom I've lavished every luxury since you were a baby, and in whom I thought I saw your mother's image. You nearly drove me mad to-night with your base ingratitude—you, an aristocrat, preferring the hireling to the master—spitting on the old man who wanted to make you his darling, and mocking him from the arms of his servant, to whom you'll be just a young man's slave."

Dorsay spoke very quietly and slowly, and there was something almost like tears in his voice. Both John and Elsie could not help noticing that he seemed to hobble rather than walk as he left the lounge. He seemed, too, as if he had grown terribly old and grey all of a sudden.

"I can't help feeling a little sorry for him," she confided to John when they were alone.

"He had no earthly right to go on as he *did,*" replied her lover. "His conduct was unbelievable."

"Still, I hope he isn't really injured or something," replied Elsie.

"I don't think so, dearest," said John: "a little shaken, no doubt, but not really hurt. He's got the strength of a man of thirty."

"Yes, he is very strong," said Elsie. "There was a time when it was said that he could pick a man up with his teeth."

"Good Lord, just as well that time is over or where should I be?"

"Never mind that, dearest, it's all over. You've won, and you're my great big cave-man from now on."

"But Elsie dearest, how are we going to live? I've no job now remember."

"Great big silly. I've got five thousand pounds."

"But sweetheart, how can I live on you?"

"Whoever said you were going to?"

"But I've got no money at all except my last month's salary."

"No, but you will have. Listen, I've got a brilliant idea for your future career my love. Did you take a degree at Oxford?"

"No worse luck. Father was ruined before my second year was out."

"That means you have one more year to go. We'd better live at Oxford and you'd better finish off your B.A. there as a non-collegiate student."

"How do you know that can be done?"

"Looked it all up in the library weeks and weeks ago—directly I knew we'd got that five thousand. It can be done and it shall. By the way, what were you going to do after you had left college if things hadn't gone wrong?"

"I was thinking of being ordained."

"Well you can still be ordained. And then you will get a nice Parish to be Curate in, and you won't be living on me at all. You can even pay me back out of your stipend if you're as proud as all that. And how's that for a great scheme? No refusal now—it's as much for me as for you. If you turn me down because of that five thousand pounds I'll burn it: so there!"

It is perhaps unnecessary to relate that Tarren agreed to the proposition above unfolded, and so the lovers retired for the night in a comparatively happy frame of mind. As they bid one another good-night—or rather good morning, it being nearly a quarter to four—Elsie said to John in an undertone—

"You don't really think Sir Charles means to send for the police in the morning do you dearest?"

"I shouldn't think so, sweetheart," was his reply. "You see he really deserved all he got, and I think he knows that too well to rake the matter up again. He'll be quiet enough, never fear."

Elsie smiled, and lifted up her face to be kissed. Tarren took the fullest advantage of the invitation, and it was nearly five minutes later that he disappeared along the corridor, and Elsie, after watching him out of sight round the corner, slipped into her room.

The darkness was just beginning to fade as she slipped between the sheets. But, although she was thoroughly exhausted with the night's happenings, she found it all but impossible to sleep. Some instinct seemed to tell her that the events of that evening were not over yet: she felt an uncomfortable foreboding that there was a sequel which was yet to come.

Several times she dozed off, only to wake again with a start and listen intently before settling down again although only to toss to and fro. Her fitful intervals of slumber were disturbed and broken by horrible dreams—or rather by a kind of dream-fugue with Sir Charles' face, as it looked in that dreadful moment when she had woken up in John's arms and found him staring at them, for a theme. First she just dreamed that she and John were re-acting over again that awful scene in the lounge: then that John and Dorsay were fighting, and that Dorsay lay dead, and John had killed him: then she dreamed again, after the relief of a few minutes wakefulness, and this time that her last dream was quite true: that it was morning, and the police had come to arrest John for murder: murder that she declared him to be quite innocent of. Then she dreamed that she was dreaming that John had murdered Dorsay, and that she awoke from her dream dream to find that Dorsay had killed John and had mocked her by pretending to have been killed himself.

Then, in her dream, Sir Charles came to her room and told her that John had run away from her and that she belonged to him. She could see the horrible leer on his face as he bent over her, and she turned to run from him and she ran in her sleep madly until she thought she was on the edge of a precipice: she saw it and stopped dead in her flight, but Dorsay ran on and slipping fell over the edge, catching her by the hand as he fell and dragging her over. With a scream she thought she went over the edge. She was falling down, down, down, *down—crash.*

With one fearful scream she woke up to find herself in bed still, and alone. So it was all a dream—thank God.

With a sigh of relief she settled herself down in bed, and, as she still felt nervous, she switched on the electric light. She looked at the clock on the table at her bedside. She had only been in bed three-quarters of an hour. Heavens, it seemed she must have been sleeping and dreaming horrible things for nights on end.

She lay awake and watched the pale blue-grey of early dawn creep through her window, and felt glad the day was breaking. Fainter and fainter grew the electric lamp, until, at last, it was eclipsed by the rising sun. By this time Elsie's over-excited brain had calmed down, and her tired body had its way. She was fast asleep—buried in as sound and dreamless a slumber as if she were a child of six without a care in the world.

It must have been well past eleven o'clock in the morning when Elsie was awakened by a violent hammering at her bedroom door. She got hurriedly out of bed, seized a dressing-gown, stuck her bare feet into a pair of slippers, and unlocked the door. Corbin stood outside looking ghastly white and shaking with fear.

"Why, Corbin, what's the matter?" she asked in alarm.

It was some seconds before the man could reply to her question. Then—"Quick, Miss Elsie," he said, in a hoarse, trembling voice. "They want you downstairs at once—"

"Want me downstairs? Who is it wants me downstairs?"

"The . . . *police,* Miss Elsie . . ."

Elsie turned deathly white. The police! So Sir Charles had kept his word after all. Poor John! What a horrible ordeal for him.

She was just about to tell the butler curtly that she would be ready shortly when the man finished his sentence:—

"Sir Charles was murdered in the night."

CHAPTER V

SMALL WONDER CORBIN TREMBLED and looked pale. He had personally made the discovery that his master's none too creditable career had come to a violent end in the night.

As usual he had risen about eight that morning with the other members of the household staff, and had busied himself for the first hour or two of the day with various small matters to which it was his duty to attend. He had not given so much as a thought to the happenings of the previous evening. He was much too used to his employer's little ways; and, since he had been in Sir Charles' service for some ten years, he had seen many a worse drunken brawl than the last.

He felt though a glow of satisfaction at the knowledge that John Tarren was to leave "Dorsay Hall" in disgrace; since he viewed Elsie's lover with that particular form of dislike with which many of his class regard people who, while happening to be noticeably above them in rank and origin, happen also to be conspicuously poorer, or at least quite as poor; and so, while not a source of tips or wages, have as many social privileges as if they were.

About ten o'clock on that fateful morning Corbin recalled that Sir Charles had instructed him to see that he had a cup of tea sent up to him at ten-thirty precisely, and so he at once gave Mary Pane, the housemaid, instructions that this order was to be duly carried out. The lady in question had a rooted objection to going anywhere near Sir Charles, which dated from a certain lurid occasion some six or eight months previously, and told Corbin as much, refusing point-blank to go alone and unprotected to the baronet's decidedly unchaste resting-place. Corbin appreciated very well indeed the wisdom of her unwillingness, and so took the tray from her and carried it up himself. Getting no answer to several knocks, he opened the door of the bedroom and, of course, discovered that the bed had not been slept in.

Mr. Corbin was not at all disturbed at this discovery. Sir Charles' bed very frequently was *not* slept in. There was, of course, the fact that the baronet had himself ordered the tea to be sent to this very room at this very hour, but as Dorsay—save on those very rare occasions when he was quite sober—not infrequently gave orders the sense of which nobody could see but himself, even this suggested nothing to the butler's mind. He just put the tray down on a table beside the bed and looked at his watch to make sure he had made no mistake about the hour, and finding that he was not before, but a little after, his time, picked up the tea and went back to the kitchen. He would try again in half an hour's time.

The explanation of Sir Charles' bed being undisturbed at a time when that worthy was not away from home which suggested itself to Mr. Corbin's mind was a delightfully simple one. There had been a new, and young, and very pretty, kitchen-maid engaged a few days before. She had arrived last evening, and Dorsay, being a thoughtful employer, anxious for his servants' welfare, not infrequently made a personal enquiry as to the comfort of the quarters allotted to them on such occasions.

Unhappily this excellent idea was rather upset; for, when Corbin arrived again in the servants' quarters, not only did he learn on discreet enquiry that the pretty kitchenmaid had been up since six A.M., and that her room had been "done" hours ago, but Mary Pane informed him that the library door was locked from the inside and it was impossible to get any answer no matter how one knocked.

A moment's reflection, and the whole thing was as clear as day to the powerful intellect of Mr. Walter Corbin. He remembered the previous evening's instructions about refilling the whisky decanter in the library. Of course! It had all happened before. Sir Charles had been "on the binge" all night, and doubtless was at that very moment in that exceptionally heavy slumber which always followed on all-night interview with Mr. Johnny Walker. It was a pity he had locked himself in though. Perhaps he would sleep for several more hours, and, in any case, waking him up on these festive occasions was a matter calling for great discretion, as the lord and master of "Dorsay Hall" had as a rule a decidedly "Mondayish" feeling when he was roused, and the bold Prince Charming who awoke this particular "Sleeping Beauty" was far more likely to be rewarded with a kick than with a kiss. Even if the member of the household who undertook this fearsome task happened to be one of the fair sex the whole affair had a painful resemblance to "Beauty and the Beast"—only without the happy ending.

Still, someone had to do the job since, if the master of the house were allowed to sleep his sleep right out, and woke up of his own accord, he might, quite probably, make enquiries as to why he had not been roused before, and Corbin, standing higher in Dorsay's favour than any other servant, took the duty upon himself.

After knocking violently upon the library door without result, and calling out loudly without receiving any answer, Corbin thought of a brilliant idea. He went to the telephone in the lounge, and, after requesting the operator to give him a ring, connected the instrument with the phone standing on the desk in the library. The exchange rang and rang for some minutes but nothing happened. So, after thanking the girl for her trouble, the butler thought he would go round to the french windows of the library, and attempt to look into the room to make sure Dorsay was really there, and had not gone out somewhere in the night. The curtains might be drawn, but, on the other hand, they might not as Sir Charles had a habit of sitting in the library without covering the windows.

A trifle nervously Corbin put this project into execution. When he arrived outside the french windows, however, he was amazed to find them gaping wide open. A moment later, and he very nearly fainted. And well he might, for a sight met his eyes which would have horrified a very much more hardened observer than he.

Practically the whole surface of the writing-table, which stood in the centre of the room, was covered with great gouts and clots of blood, some of which was dripping in thick sticky splotches on to the carpet. Sprawling in the swivel-chair at this gruesome desk was a figure in dress clothes which the butler immediately identified as what had once been Sir Charles Dorsay, although for anybody not quite so well acquainted with the man it would not have been so easy a task, because the greater part of the head had been blown away, evidently by the close discharge of both barrels of a large-bore shot-gun which lay, where it had apparently fallen after the tragedy, on the floor beside the chair. One arm of the body hung limply downwards as if it had dropped the gun from its lifeless fingers, and the other was flung across the table where the hand still clasped an old book bound in what looked like discoloured pigskin. All that remained of the face lay on the blotting-pad which was dyed crimson from corner to corner, and comprised nothing more than a sickening pulp of scorched flesh blackened with burned gun-powder. In more than one place the skull had been exposed to view, and charred chips of bone mingled with stray scraps of some quite indescribable greyish-red matter, which the horrified butler supposed to be fragments of brain, lay round about the room. A positive swarm of flies and bluebottles buzzed busily round the loathsome mass of mortality at the table. Only twelve hours before the place had been a library. Now it was a charnel house of death in its most loathsome form.

All this Corbin took in with one horrified glance. For a second he stared stupidly at the dreadful spectacle as though it were some disgustful daydream. Then, when the sense-paralysis of shock had worn off a little and realisation dawned, a strangled oath broke from his lips, and he turned and fled back into the garden. He had seen the key in the lock of the library door, but he could not for the life of him pass the table. All he wanted was to put as great a distance as possible between himself and that *thing*: to get the filthy smell of gunpowder and blood out of his nostrils, and the maddening drone of those carrion-insects out of his ears.

Out once again in the sunshine it was fully ten minutes before Corbin had recovered himself sufficiently to think. Then a jumbled rush of fearsome impressions flooded in his mind. Sir Charles Dorsay was nothing to him: the mere fact that the man was dead affected him no more than the death of a stray dog would have done save that it lost him his job. But to have been suddenly confronted with that which was in the library: to have seen that vile thing with his own eyes: to have been the first to discover that there had been murder done: murder, too, of an unthinkably foul sort: to know that damnable corpse was lying there crying to the world for vengeance, and demanding a human sacrifice as the price of its blood: to have actually been on the premises when the crime had been committed, and so to be among those persons upon whom the machinery of justice could not fail to cast suspicion of his being implicated, struck a wild terror to his very soul.

Suppose, suppose, there should be some mistake, suppose his footprints on the carpet near the french windows, suppose something however slight should draw him into the net of the police? Suppose he should be called upon to pay for the life of his late employer? Such legal blunders had occurred in the past, he knew, and would doubtless occur again. In his young days he had once seen a man whom he knew to be guiltless condemned to death for the murder of a rich merchant. He had been too great a moral coward to come forward with his evidence for the good reason that the real criminal had threatened him with death if he should pass on to anyone what he had seen of the affair, and he remembered the victim's terrible agonised stare as he was led away to his cell. Suppose the wheel should have turned and he, Corbin, be in the place of that man he had allowed to perish in order to save his own skin? Beads of cold sweat stood on his forehead at the bare idea and his teeth rattled in his head. It might come to pass: it might. And, if it did, how could he, a penniless wanderer, hire a costly barrister to prove his innocence—a Counsel who to save him must needs be a man more skilled than the brilliant advocate who would be generously paid out of the comparatively bottomless coffers of the State to put a rope round his neck? Who cared if an unemployed domestic servant lived or died!

All this went through Corbin's mind in a few seconds, and galvanised him to immediate action. For one moment he thought he would run away as fast as his coward legs could carry him, but he quickly saw the folly of such an act. It would make him look like the guilty person at once, and, since he was really quite without any shadow of blame in the matter, perhaps, after all, he had little or nothing to fear. He decided, therefore, that he would get into touch with the police immediately, and set the law in motion himself. Surely this would do more than anything else to safeguard him from suspicion.

Mopping the cold sweat from his icy brow with his pocket handkerchief, the butler hastened across the tennis-lawn through the flower-garden back to the West wing which contained the Servants' Hall. As soon as he entered the place again he was accosted by Mary Pane.

"Well?" she questioned, "did he blow you up very bad?" and then, as she saw Corbin's ghastly; face, she added— "Coo! Mr. Corbin. You don't 'alf look bad! Wot's 'e bin sayin'?" and, turning to the kitchenmaid, who had run up eager for news as to in what frame of mind the butler had found, "The Guv'nor," she said sotto voce:—"Blow me if I don't think he's given 'im the sack . . . great shame . . . ought to be ashamed of 'isself . . . didn't ought to carry on as 'e did . . . I'd tell 'im straight I would, etc., etc."

Corbin managed to find a chair, and dropped heavily into it. He was quite unconscious of anything beyond a general sympathetic buzz of women's voices round him. Black spots floated before his eyes. Then, remembering his decision, he pulled himself together with an effort—just as Mary Pane was bending over him and saying:

"What's the matter now? . . . come on . . . I tell us . . . we'll all stand up for you you know . . . we won't stand for it . . . if you gotta go we goes with you . . . don't take it to 'art so . . . why bless yer 'e'll come round when 'is mind clears and forget 'e ever told yer to go."

Corbin staggered to his feet. "I've not got the sack," he rasped in a voice he would not have known as his own—"It's the Guv'nor . . . Sir Charles . . . 'e . . . 'e . . ."

"Wot's up with 'im? Got D.T.'s again and given yer a start?"

Corbin licked his dry and cracked hps. "Give me some water," he said. Then, as Mary lingered without doing any-thing, he grew irritated, and shouted, or rather croaked, out—"Hurry woman! I can't stand gossiping here . . . I've got to fetch the police at once!"

"Police! What for?"

Corbin opened his mouth several times without any sound resulting: but at length he gasped the fatal words . . .

"It's Sir Charles . . . 'e's . . . *dead!*"

"Oo—err!!!" The maid pressed forward with gruesome curiosity. " 'Is 'art?"

"Nar—'e was *murdered.* Shot with one of 'is own guns!"

Of course, there was a fearful commotion at this piece of information. But Corbin had no time to worry about that. He dashed from the kitchen into the hall, and seizing the tele-phone, was through to the police in a few seconds. He gave every detail he could, and was told, of course, that the matter would be seen to immediately. Scotland Yard would be in the place in about an hour. Meanwhile nothing was to be touched, and no one was to leave on any pretence whatever.

Next he got through to a doctor, and then as soon as he felt the responsibility of the affair some what off his shoul-ders he bethought himself of the events of the night before. He had heard every detail of the quarrel, for what happened after he left the room when the actual struggle between Tar-ren and Dorsay had begun he had been careful to overhear by keeping within earshot until he had deemed it wise to return to the lounge.

John Tarren had been sacked on account of his affair with Elsie Mervyn with whom Sir Charles had been in love. He was quite penniless, and Elsie would lose something like a quarter of a million pounds by marrying him against Dorsay's will. She had apparently been quite determined to do so, and so Sir Charles had avowed his intention of altering his will and so cutting her off with a shilling—or rather with her mother's five thousand pounds. Now although five thousand pounds was better than nothing it was not anything like a quarter of a million plus a valuable estate within a few miles of London. If Dorsay could have been prevented from making the fatal alteration in his will, Elsie would inherit his every penny at his death. The old man was inflexible, and hated Tarren from the bottom of his heart, so there would be only one way in which he could have been prevented from carrying out his threat. And that one way had been effected in the most brutal of ways. Elsie Mervyn was now mistress of the place and of every cent Dorsay had in the world as well as of her own five thousand pounds. And who would derive the most benefit from her legacy?—why John Tarren, of course. "Hence," reasoned Corbin, "doubtless John Tarren is the murderer—what a fool I've been—why didn't I think of that before?" But how would Tarren get away with it? Easily enough. He would swear to Elsie that he was not guilty. She had five thousand pounds in the next day or so of her own—apart from the dead man's estate. That five thousand would be used to fight the case for her lover. He could and would brief the best Counsel in the country; and, naturally enough, since money always talks—and there was no lack of ready cash to say nothing of more to follow—he would be acquitted, and the death of Sir Charles explained away as "suicide while of an unsound mind." Everybody too knew that Dorsay was very upset at Elsie's point-blank refusal to marry him, and enraged and broken-hearted at her preferring the secretary. Here was a first-class motive for suicide!

Corbin was no fool. He had knocked about the world for forty-nine odd years and seen some four countries. What he lacked in mental cultivation and character he made up for in shrewdness and experience of life, and so he managed in this way to put two and two together, and came definitely to the conclusion that Tarren had killed his master to prevent his sweetheart from being disinherited. And really the thing did seem possible when regarded from the standpoint of cold-blooded reason. Equally reasonable seemed the suicide theory. But Mr. Corbin, as we have remarked before, hated Tarren and would have preferred things to point to the theory most likely to send that worthy to the scaffold. And to show how clear-headed Mr. Corbin was—now that the chances of the blame falling on his own shoulders seemed almost past—he contemplated the prospect of helping to weave a mesh round Tarren that would send him to the gallows with that calm sense of public duty which great men always experience when doing their bit in helping to destroy an enemy—especially when that enemy happens never to have done them any harm beyond occupying a position in life superior to their own.

"Yes," he thought, "no doubt about it," as he poured himself out a stiff tot of brandy, "Tarren's done and bunked off." He was just about to go upstairs and see for himself if John had actually "bunked off," as he put it, when no less a person than John himself entered the lounge, coolly puffing a morning cigarette. He saw Corbin long before Corbin saw him, and, even if he remembered the man's veiled insults of the night before, he showed no resentment, since he sang out "Good morning, Corbin: I'm a bit late to-day I'm afraid, but so apparently is everybody else: breakfast ready?"

This was a remarkably casual and cool greeting from a man who had—according to the thinking of Mr. Walter Corbin—murdered his employer in the night, and apparently the butler thought so, for he looked long and curiously at John before replying—"I suppose you don't know it yet Mr. Tarren, but Sir Charles was murdered—or committed suicide—in the night. The whole place is in a terrible upset."

"Good God! Murdered? Suicide? How?"

"Shot in the face by one of his own guns."

"What a dreadful thing—who discovered it?"

"I had the bad luck to. Fairly turned me sick—face was blown to a pulp."

"What a terrible thing—but surely it couldn't have been a murder. He must have committed suicide—surely he must."

"Looked more like murder to me."

"Have you sent for the police?"

"Yes—they'll be here soon."

"Does Miss Mervyn know yet?"

"No. She's not up."

"Poor girl, What a terrible shock it will be for her." Corbin looked narrowly at John from the corners of his small, close-set eyes, as he said very meaningly, as if to show that John's calm manner did not deceive him in the least:

"It'll be a very serious shock for anybody who stands to get something by it, I'm thinking—and the police'll see it is too!"

Tarren looked Corbin straight in the eyes as he replied sharply: "What do you mean?"

What Corbin meant was pretty obvious to both men, but the former never had the opportunity to be more lucid as there was a violent knocking on the front-door.

Without more apology than a grunt, half nervous, and half of satisfaction, Corbin went to open the door.

The police had arrived, and were duly ushered into the lounge where John waited for them, still smoking his cigarette steadily, a trifle pale, but quite collected.

Corbin, on the contrary, as soon as he was faced by the living representatives of law and order, lost his newly-acquired nerve as quickly as he had found it. He was pale and trembling as he answered the first questions of the Detective-Inspector who had been put in charge of the case, and spoke in a low uneven voice. He stressed his horror at finding his employer dead, and insisted on his innocence with an agonized inability to say barely anything more than "I assure you sir—on my oath, sir—I know nothing about it—Sir Charles was the best of masters, sir—I know you won't suspect me, sir—I'd rather die than kill anybody sir—" and similar ejaculations, until, to a less keen observer of human nature than Detective-Inspector Richardson, he would most certainly have given the impression that if he was not actually guilty, at least he knew more about the case than he should.

As it was he was just told sharply that nobody suspected him, and that no innocent person had anything to fear, and instructed to conduct the Inspector and the constables at once to the library where the murdered man lay.

"Spare me, sir," implored Corbin, "I'd rather . . . not . . . go . . . there if I can help it . . . it horrifies me sir even to think of what is in there," and then, turning to Tarren, asked him, or rather implored him, in a very different tone from that which he had ever before used to Dorsay's secretary, to deputise for him in the matter, saying to the Inspector: "Here is Mr. Tarren, sir . . . Mr. John Tarren he was poor Sir Charles' secretary, sir . . . he will, I am sure, take you into the library, sir . . . Mr. Tarren, sir . . . you won't refuse me, I feel ill . . . too . . . ill and sick, sir, to go there again . . ."

Of course, John agreed, although he did not welcome the idea of looking on the dead man who had apparently been so horribly murdered, and was seemingly so dreadful to look on. He offered the Inspector a cigarette, which he accepted, and then asked him to come along to the library where the dead man lay.

Richardson instructed Corbin to assemble the entire household in the lounge while he was making the preliminary inspection of the victim. Corbin departed on this comparatively welcome mission, and John Tarren, not without some internal qualms since he had only seen one dead man before in his life—his father who had died peaceably in his bed—led the representatives of Scotland Yard to the room of death.

CHAPTER VI

WHEN ELSIE HEARD THE DREADFUL NEWS she could barely credit her ears. The ground seemed to give way under her feet for a moment, and she would, in all probability, have fallen had she not gripped the door to save herself.

Sir Charles Dorsay had meant very little to her in terms of affection for as long as she could remember. And of late years she had both loathed and feared the man—for the best of reasons, too. Although she was the nearest approach to kith and kin that the baronet had possessed, yet she could hardly bring herself to mourn his death in the least—as she would, doubtless, have done had their relationship been different.

But for the man to be murdered: for him to meet his end so suddenly: to be butchered under his own roof in the dead of night: it was unspeakable, and terrified her almost to the point of stupor, and the knowledge that the fearful tragedy which had cast its black wings over "Dorsay Hall" without the remotest warning had claimed as its victim the man whom she regarded as the evil genius of the household, rather increased than diminished her horror.

She was almost on the point of launching a thousand and one questions at the butler when a glance at his starting eyes and deathly face told her it would be better to refrain. She would hear the ghastly details soon enough.

Mustering all her courage she told Corbin she would hurry down, and started to make a hasty toilet her mind working rapidly the while in spite of her every effort to avoid thinking of the matter.

Murdered! It was a terrible word. But how had Sir Charles been murdered—how? That the man possessed many enemies she felt certain. But which of them could have done this thing? It frightened her to death. Or stay, had Dorsay really been the victim of an assassin? What about the possibility of suicide? She remembered her guardian's recent threats of self-destruction. Had he really kept his word and taken his own life? And, if he had, would it not be for no better reason than because she had refused to marry him? Horrible thought! Could it really be that the old man's blood was in this way upon her hands? She would not be the first woman to have sent a man to his grave truly; but, all the same, the idea made her shudder, and there came into her mind a regret, faint it is true, but still a distinct regret, that she should have spoken to Sir Charles in the way she did the night before. Perchance it had been those hasty trenchant words of hers that had brought about this living nightmare. She called to mind how old and grey he had looked when last she saw him—at the moment when he had hobbled to the library to alter his will.

His will . . . ah . . . his will . . . a quarter of a million . . . men had been murdered for lesser sums than that times without number. Could someone have killed him because of this money?—or killed him to prevent that alteration in his will? Suppose—Oh God—suppose John had . . . but no . . . no . . . he was incapable of it . . . incapable of it . . . unless . . . dreadful thought . . . there had been another altercation between the two men after she had gone to bed . . . an altercation about the will, and they had come again to blows as they did in the lounge before her very eyes . . . and then . . . then . . . in the heat of the moment . . .

She buried her face in her hands. Merciful Heavens! It could not be—it could not—unless . . . Dorsay's death had been the direct or indirect result of the struggle . . . he was an old man and a sudden stroke . . . heart failure . . . a thousand things . . . Or even if the dispute had come to a head in her presence was it not just possible that the tussle had told upon the older man, and this the unlooked for, fearful, result. And if so . . . what of John? Would the police hold him answerable for his employer's death?

What was to be done?

She knew that she might be simply torturing herself for nothing. The whole thing might be an accident, ordinary heart failure, death from alcoholic poisoning, or suicide, for which it would be impossible to blame anyone. But the dread of anything in the inquest, she knew to be inevitable, pointing to Tarren as the culprit, or even as being the direct cause of the tragedy, haunted her persistently as she huddled on her clothes and dashed a brush dipped in cold water over her hair.

When she arrived downstairs she found the whole house permeated with that peculiar gloom one always associates with the presence of death as well as with an atmosphere of strain and nightmarish suspense. The police had taken possession of the place, converting it from an English country house, with all its homely dignity, to a kind of temporary jail in which the prisoners had their nerves wracked by a miserable uncertainty as to whether they were shortly to be released or to be condemned either as murderers or accessories to murder.

There was a constable on duty in the great hall, who told her that Detective-Inspector Richardson awaited her in the lounge. Here she found the rest of the household assembled in a nervous bunch in the corner of the room farthest from the library door, from behind which came a murmur of men's voices. John she noticed was missing, and her heart seemed nearly to jump into her mouth.

"Where is Mr. Tarren?" she asked the housemaid. "In the library with the Scotland Yard gentleman, Miss Elsie," was the reply.

Elsie heaved a sigh of relief. It was apparently all right then as far as John was concerned. Then, with a sick shudder, she remembered what apparently lay behind that door over there and asked, "Is . . . poor Sir Charles in there?"

"Yes, Miss—'e's in there—they're examining 'im—Dr. Horton's there as well."

"How did he die, Mary?" Elsie asked in a trembling voice.

" 'E was shot dead, Miss—shot in the 'ead, Miss, with one of them sporting guns in there."

"Was it suicide?"

The maid drew Elsie aside, and, lowering her voice to a stage whisper, replied,

" 'E wos murdered! Mr. Corbin said it wearn't 'umanly possible fer 'im to 'ave shot hisself—that is like he's bin shot. It's the most 'orrible sight Mr. Corbin was tellin' me—orl 'is 'ead blown away an' 'is brains and 'is blood orl aver the room. 'E's bin murdered in 'is bed—and its come as a judgment on 'im."

"Did the police say so?"

"They 'aven't said notliink yet, Miss Elsie."

Just as Elsie was about to open her mouth, the door of the library opened about half-way and John Tarren came out followed by a short bullet-headed man in a dark tweed suit, who quickly shut the door behind him, and locked it putting the key into his pocket.

Elsie rushed to her lover, who put his arm protectingly round her.

"Oh, John—it's like a nightmare, I can hardly believe it. Is it really true that Sir Charles has been murdered?"

"He's been killed somehow, darling—but we don't know more yet, there's a doctor in there now making a careful examination. He may be able to help us find out."

Here the bullet-headed man broke in: "Is this Miss Mervyn, the dead man's ward?"

"Yes," replied John. "Elsie dear, this is Detective-Inspector Richardson of Scotland Yard who is in charge of this dreadful business."

Richardson bowed a trifle stiffly. "Sorry we have to meet under such trying conditions, Miss Mervyn," said he. "If you don't mind taking a seat, I should like to ask you a few questions which may help us in clearing up the death of your late guardian."

Elsie sat down as she was told, and replied, a little shakily: "Of course, anything I can do to help I shall be only too pleased to do. Was he really—murdered do you think?"

"I can't say yet, can't say at all. It might be anything. Murder, suicide, or purely an accident. It all depends on what comes to light. Can you personally suggest any reason why he should want to commit suicide?"

Elsie was about to speak, then hesitated. Richardson noticed this immediately and said, quite sharply:

"Go on—why do you hesitate—can you call to mind any motive for suicide—think carefully, and remember there's nothing to be gained by holding anything back. It will have to come out in the end, whatever it may be."

Elsie saw at once by the man's manner that it would be worse than useless to attempt to conceal Sir Charles' recent attitude to herself and to Tarren. Corbin would be sure to be questioned, and she shuddered to think what his version of the tale might be. And, really, since Dorsay had actually threatened suicide more than once it seemed to her more than probable that he had put his threat into execution.

"As a matter of fact," she said to Richardson, trying to speak as though her heart were not racing with terror like a steam engine, "poor Sir Charles has several times threatened to kill himself."

"Why?"

"He asked me to marry him, and I refused."

"I see. When was this—recently?"

"No—several months ago." Richardson grunted. "You refused him I take it because you preferred Mr. Tarren?"

"Yes."

"Did he know that Mr. Tarren was his successful rival?"

"Not then—not until a long time afterwards."

"How long afterwards?"

"Quite a long time."

"So you said before, but surely you can be more definite. How long has Dorsay known of your relationship with Mr. Tarren?"

"We neither of us really know. He may have known for weeks, but we were not certain he knew until last night."

"Ah. Now we are getting somewhere. He found out last night did he?"

Elsie felt herself colouring under the detective's steady gaze. She hardly knew her own voice when at last she answered "Yes."

The Inspector made a brief note in his book, and then said to her, "And how did he take it when he found out?"

"He was rather upset I think . . . he—"

"You *think*. Don't you know?"

"Well you see. Inspector, when he found this out he had been drinking rather heavily, and I'm sure he was not responsible—"

"How did he find this out?"

"He came home unexpectedly and caught us together in here . . ."

"Love-making?"

"Well . . . yes . . . I suppose so."

"What did he say to you?"

"O, please don't ask that—really I can't remember—he was not in the least himself."

"I'm sorry Miss Mervyn but I must know all about this. Do try to think carefully—what did he say to you, was he angry, upset, or what?"

"He was angry, terribly angry . . ."

"Did he again threaten to kill himself?"

"No."

"Well, what did he say then?"

"He was furiously angry, and said horrible things . . ."

"What things?"

"I'd much rather forget them—he was not himself you know . . . he . . ."

"I'm afraid I must insist that you tell me what he said?"

"He insulted us horribly."

"In what way?"

"He hinted that we had been carrying on . . . immorally."

"And you hadn't?"

"O, no, no . . . we wouldn't . . . we . . ."

"I see. Well, what happened next?"

"I hardly know. It's all like a horrible dream."

"Did your lover resent this insinuation on the part of his employer?"

"Yes he did. He told him it was not true."

"There was a terrific row no doubt."

"Yes." Elsie's voice sunk into a whisper. "And did this . . . row . . . end in Sir Charles Dorsay going off to the library to make an alteration in his will?"

Elsie clutched her chair with both hands and the room seemed swimming before her eyes. Had the Inspector been questioning Corbin? she wondered to herself—where was all this cross-examination leading. Richardson's hard voice broke through her thoughts with:—

"Would you mind answering my question please? I have told you already that it is hopeless to attempt to conceal anything.

"Did Sir Charles Dorsay say he would alter his will?"

"What makes you ask that?" questioned Elsie in spite of herself. How could he possibly know?

"He was evidently engaged in drafting a will when he was shot," came the reply, "we found the half-finished draft on his desk."

Elsie pulled herself together with an effort "You are quite right, Inspector," said she. "Sir Charles did say he would alter his will last night."

"And, of course, in your disfavour. Under the old will I suppose you came in for a pretty good legacy didn't you?"

"Yes. He had left me everything."

"So you stood to lose a fortune by refusing to marry Dorsay and taking up with his secretary?"

"Yes I did. But that mattered little or nothing to me. I care nothing for money."

"And what about Mr. Tarren? Did he care at all?"

"Oh, no, no. The idea of my money never entered his head."

"But he knew you were an heiress, I suppose?"

"He may have done. But I *know* that wouldn't have influenced him in the least. He wanted me because he loved me— and still does."

John was about to break into a passionate confirmation of Elsie's last words when Richardson held up his hand.

"One at a time Mr. Tarren if you please. Now Miss Mervyn will you just tell me if, apart from your expectations under your guardian's will, you have any means or not?"

"Certainly," replied Elsie, seeing that she could create a favourable impression, and rejoicing at the opportunity—as she felt that all her other evidence had tended to put a rope round poor John's neck—"I have money of my own—quite apart from Sir Charles Dorsay's fortune."

"How much?"

"Five thousand pounds."

"I see. And from where does this fortune come?"

"From my dead mother—or rather stepmother—it was being held in trust for me by Sir Charles until I should be of age."

"And when will you be of age?"

"In four days' time now."

"Did Mr. Tarren know you had this money when he asked you to marry him?"

"Certainly not, I didn't tell him anything about it," she retorted, flushing hotly. She saw the detective smile grimly to himself as he noted down this fact; and then, suddenly realising that she had, perhaps, given an impression she did not mean to, she added quickly:—"but I told him all about it last night after the quarrel."

Richardson looked up.

"You did, did you?" Then, finishing his notes, he said to her a trifle sharply:—"What time would it be when last you saw Sir Charles alive?"

"About half-past three in the morning I think."

"The row was all over then?"

"Yes."

"And you saw Dorsay go off to the library to cut you out of his will?"!

"Yes."

"What did you do then, did you try to persuade . . . your guardian to forgive your preferring Mr. Tarren?"

"Oh no—it would have been quite useless. Sir Charles was a very hard man."

"Well, so you let him go off to do his worst?"

"Yes."

"And then?"

"I went to bed."

"Did you hear any noise in the night? That gun must have been heard a mile away. Both barrels had been fired at once."

"I woke up about a quarter to five after a horrible dream which ended by my seeming to fall into an abyss. It must have been the report of the gun that awakened me as I seem to remember hearing a crash, although, when I woke, I thought it part of my dream."

"Did you make any enquiries as to what caused the noise?"

"No. I just turned over and went to sleep again. I did not wake until the butler knocked at my door and told me the dreadful news about poor Sir Charles."

"Thanks. I don't think I need ask you any more, Miss Mervyn," said Richardson. Then, turning to John, he said;— "Now let's have your version please, Mr. Tarren. Tell me, did you hear this noise last night—or rather early this morning?"

"Yes," answered John. "The report of the gun woke me up with a jump."

"Did you try to find out what it was all about?"

"No. I didn't even look at the time. I didn't bother."

"Why?"

"I thought it was a picture falling or something of the sort. Also it's quite usual for Sir Charles to knock things over at all hours of the day and night. He was a confirmed drunkard, you know."

"And he had been very drunk when you left him to go to bed?"

"Yes."

"You are engaged to Miss Mervyn, I understand?"

"Yes, I am."

"When did this engagement start?"

"Shortly after I came here to be Sir Charles' secretary."

"How long ago?"

"Several months."

"And this romance is purely . . . a love-match?"

"Certainly."

"You both of you have kept your engagement a secret from Sir Charles Dorsay?"

"Yes."

"Why? Since you tell me it was purely a love-match and so you would have cared nothing if he I had disinherited her, why did you not speak up?"

"I did not want to feel that I had been the cause of Elsie's losing her money."

"Rather an inadequate reason, Mr. Tarren, surely. Sooner or later he would have had to know even if he had not found out—and, since he is apparently a very tough nut to crack, it could have only have come to the same thing in the end. So why all the mystery?"

"I wanted to wait until I could find another post, and make her some sort of home; and, of course, until she was of age."

"You have no means other than your earnings then?"

John coloured, but replied immediately:—"None whatever."

"Did Miss Mervyn know this?"

"Yes. I told her all about my affairs when I asked her to marry me."

"And she did not mind, I suppose?"

"No."

"But she told you nothing of this independent money of hers until last night?"

"No."

"What made her tell you last night?"

"She did not tell me directly at all."

"How do you mean?"

"I mean that when Dorsay told her that he would cut her out of his will she replied that she did not mind in the least as she had discovered that her mother had provided for her and that the money would come to her on her twenty-first birth-day."

"Did she say how she had found all this out?"

"Yes. She had been going through some papers of Sir Charles."

"And I suppose when you heard this it was news to you?"

"I don't know what you mean at all."

"I mean that if Miss Mervyn could get access to those papers I should think that you as the man's private secretary could have had ample opportunity of looking them through."

"Look here, Inspector," said John, firing up, "really if you . . ."

Richardson interrupted him. "Don't excite yourself, please," he said coldly, "but give me a direct answer, did you in point of fact know that Miss Mervyn was heiress to five thousand pounds over and above her expectations from her guardian before she spoke of it to Dorsay in your presence last night?"

"I did not."

"Sure?"

"Quite sure."

Richardson eyed John closely for a moment, and, seeing that his suspicious gaze was met steadily without so much as the flicker of an eyelid, he seemed satisfied and continued:—

"You told me just now, Mr. Tarren, that you were trying to find another post—am I right in supposing that you have not yet been successful?"

"Yes."

"I see. And am I also right in supposing that Sir Charles Dorsay dismissed you from his service last night when he discovered your relationship with his ward?"

"You are quite right."

"When were you to leave?"

"At once."

"That means to-day?"

"Yes."

"Did Sir Charles Dorsay say that Miss Mervyn must leave here as well since her determination to marry you was unalterable?"

"No. Certainly not. He never hinted at such a thing."

"She could stay as long as she liked?"

"Yes."

Here Elsie broke in, "Yes, but I intended, and still intend, to go away just as soon as I come of age and can claim my money."

Richardson turned to her sharply. "Did you tell him that?"

"Yes I did," she answered almost defiantly.

"Humph! Was he upset about your determination?"

"Not particularly."

"But he felt it no doubt—since as he did not turn you out with Mr. Tarren he must still have been fond of you."

"How could he turn Miss Mervyn out when she was his ward?" asked John hotly.

"Not till she was of age, certainly," replied the detective, "but afterwards he could do as he pleased."

"He was welcome to."

"But he never even hinted at such a thing did he?" said Richardson.

"No."

"Very well then—that surely shows he was still fond of you, still in love with you too perhaps, and so he must have felt pretty badly upset at the idea of your leaving him to marry a man with no job—even though you did have five thousand pounds of your own,"—this to Elsie.

"Look here, Inspector," said John angrily, "are you trying to suggest that we are the direct cause of Sir Charles' suicide?"

"I have said nothing of the kind," answered Richardson, "nor have I made up my mind it is suicide at all yet."

"But it must be," retorted John, "what else could it be?"

Richardson shrugged his shoulders, "Murder—or possibly an accident."

"But who would murder him for Heaven's sake?"

"Plenty of people, if they had reason to."

A horrible suspicion crossed John's mind. "You surely don't imagine that I did it do you?" he cried, "over that beastly will of his . . . why . . ."

"I have come to no conclusion whatever."

"But good God man I . . ."

"Don't get excited," snapped Richardson, "but just answer my questions. I suppose you two are going to be married as soon as Miss Mervyn can claim her money?"

"Yes we are."

"And in the meantime what are you going to live on Mr. Tarren?"

"I have a full month's salary which was handed to me when I was dismissed last night."

"I see. Well, that's your affair, anyhow. But to revert to Sir Charles Dorsay, tell me, do you, as his private secretary know of any reason other than his disappointment over his ward's rejection of his heart and hand in your favour, why he should turn to suicide?"

"In what way?"

"Well—say financial embarrassment for instance."

"Not as far as I know, but Sir Charles was very secretive about money matters. He has, I believe, several banking accounts. All the cheques I used to draw for him to sign were ordinary domestic ones to tradesmen, or servants' wages, and were drawn on the Charing Cross branch of the London and Suburban Bank. This much I feel sure of—he was a very wealthy man; and, although he seemed to spend at a fearful rate, he never seemed to be worried about money."

"Did he gamble or bet much?"

"A good deal, I believe; but I never had anything to do with the money side of these transactions. In fact I know very little about the business side of his life at all—if I may use such a term. You see I have only been here a little over eight months, and never been taken much into his confidence."

"I see. Can you tell me who would know more?"

"His solicitor, no doubt."

"Who is his solicitor?"

"Mr. William Hampton, 34, Lincoln's Inn Fields."

"Thanks. I had better have them down here at once. Have you got their telephone-number."

John gave Richardson the required number, and he picked up the telephone to summon the family lawyers. Having got through, and being told that Mr. William Hampton was, at that moment, out; but that, as soon as be returned to the office, he would, of course, immediately put in appearance at "Dorsay Hall," the Scotland Yard man told John that he had "done with him for the moment," and Corbin was next "put to the question."

CHAPTER VII

THE BUTLER HAD BEEN STANDING well out of sight of the detective, but well in earshot of all the conversation that had taken place, and when he found that it was his turn to undergo examination at the hands of the "Cops"—whom he dreaded with that dread peculiar to men of criminal tendencies—he was by no means pleased. Although, as we all know, Mr. Corbin was quite free of all connection with the death of Dorsay, yet we may as well confess that in other respects he was not quite so stainless. Sir Charles had been a rich and lavish man. Sir Charles had been a confirmed drunkard. Corbin had been his toady-in-chief, and Prime Minister to his vices. Result—Corbin had systematically swindled his master daily throughout the year. Further, he had never been found out; for the very good reason that Dorsay had never troubled to find out where missing unopened boxes of choice Havana cigars went to: how dozens of bottles of whisky somehow melted down to one or two with a rapidity which even Sir Charles' healthy appetite for liquid refreshment could not account for: why it was that he never got any change after Corbin had run an errand unless he remembered to ask for it: and how it came about that when Corbin transferred his money from one waistcoat to another some was nearly always mysteriously missing. Further, had Dorsay actually caught Corbin in the act, it is doubtful if he would have prosecuted him, as the deceased baronet was not that kind of a man. Not he. Give the offender over to the police? Oh dear no. He would have kept him eternally on the rack of suspense, and dangled the threat of proceedings over his head day and night: played with him as a cat will play with a mouse and with even more delight: just killed him by inches for a new kind of thrill in intervals between wine and women.

Sir Charles Dorsay had a beautiful nature!

Still, as a matter of fact, it never came to this. Corbin had gathered confidence in his own smartness in leading the old fellow "up the garden" year in and year out as we already know. So it was rather a farce to be brought into direct contact with a real live detective who might bring a lot of things to light which Mr. Walter Corbin would sooner were kept well away in the dark.

Still, he had to go through with it, and pulled himself together with an effort as Richardson turned to a fresh page in his notebook.

"Now, Mr. Corbin," he began, "what time last night was it that you saw Sir Charles Dorsay alive for the last time?"

"It was about a quarter to four this morning, sir," he replied, "but a lot of things happened before then, sir, that I think you ought to know about."

"Eh?"

Both Elsie and John turned a deathly white. What was the fellow going to say?

Mr. Corbin made up his mind, as we know, that no shadow of suspicion should fall on him whatever else happened, and having noted that neither Elsie or John had mentioned the fact that Sir Charles and his secretary had come to blows thought that he might with advantage to himself bring the matter up. Experience of life taught him that when men came to blows over a woman and that woman had managed to part them they not infrequently renewed the battle when she was out of the way and carried it to a finish. So he thought he would not let the detective miss the opportunity of asking John if he had shot Dorsay in the library, not of course to "kill him wilfully with malice aforethought" but just "bump him off" semi-accidentally in the course, of a fight for the possession of the gun—or otherwise.

So, in answer to Richardson's sharp enquiry, he said:—
"You see, sir, as you've 'eard there was a row 'ere last night."

"Yes?"

"Well sir it was like this—Sir Charles was not quite his-self and Mr. Tarren's blood was up proper. So they went on at each other somethink awful—and 'ad a 'ell of a fight, sir—rolling over like dawgs tryin' to get at each other's throats they were."

Richardson turned to John. "That so?" he snapped.

John drew in a sharp breath before answering, "If you mean—'did Sir Charles and I come to blows last night'—the answer is yes."

"You did eh? Fought a man old enough to be your father?"

"I could hardly help myself."

"Did he attack you then?"

"Worse—he struck Miss Mervyn."

"He did—did he?"

"Yes—the brute—and although I had managed to keep my temper till then, that was too much and I went for him—I couldn't help it."

"And there was a violent struggle?"

"Yes."

"You got the better of it no doubt?"

"Eventually. But I had a job. He was a very powerful man. Had he been sober I could not have managed him."

"Was he badly hurt?"

"Good Lord no. He might have got a few bruises, but otherwise he seemed no worse."

"And Miss Mervyn tried to separate you when you fought?"

"Yes, I did," put in Elsie, "but . . ."

Richardson interrupted her. "Never mind 'buts' just now Miss Mervyn"—then, turning again to John, he said:—

"After the struggle was over tell me just what happened please."

"Sir Charles went off to the library saying he was about to draft out a new will; and, after a while, I went to bed as soon as I had seen Miss Mervyn to her room."

"You did not see Dorsay again alive?"

"No."

"Will you swear you did not see him alive again?"

"Yes."

"What was the first intimation you had of his death?"

"Corbin told me he was dead as soon as I got down to breakfast this morning."

"What time was that?"

"About eleven.

"You had not seen the body until you went in the library with me?"

"No."

"Thank you." Richardson turned again to Corbin. "Now Corbin," he said, "what was the very last you saw of Sir Charles alive?"

"In the library sir last night about a quarter to four: I took 'im in a fresh bottle of whisky and a glass on a tray, and he told me I could go to bed, gave orders for tea to be brought to his bedroom at half-past ten."

"Were the french windows of the room open when you went in?"

"No sir. Closed. I bolted them before I left but did not draw the curtains as Sir Charles told me not to."

"After you left did you hear the key turned in the door?"

"No sir."

"And you went straight to bed?"

"Yes sir."

"You never saw Sir Charles again alive?"

"No sir."

"And you were the first to discover that he was dead this morning?"

"Yessir."

"Now tell me just how you came to discover that?"

"Well you see sir it was I who took him up the tea this morning. I went to 'is room, and found that the bed had not been slept in. So I thought he must 'ave been up all night or something, came to the library and found the french windows open and 'im lying there dead. Give me the fair 'orrors it did!"

"You went in through the french windows?"

"Yessir."

"Did you try the door first?"

"Yessir. But it was locked. I thought he'd perhaps gone to sleep in there after lockin' hisself in, so I went round by the windows to see."

"Did you not first try to rouse him from the other side of the door—you could hardly have expected to find the windows open since you say you had locked them from inside."

"Well you see sir I knew that most like the curtains would not be drawn across so I could 'ave looked in the room."

"Why did you want to do that?"

"To see if he were in there, sir."

"You must have *known* that since the door was locked from the inside and his bed had not been slept in."

Corbin looked uncomfortable. "You see, sir, as I found I couldn't wake the master up by callin' out and hammerin' on the door, I thought, maybe, he just wouldn't answer me—he was like that sometimes when 'e didn't want to be disturbed—or 'e'd gone to sleep and couldn't 'ear. And then sir 'e 'ad been very drunk last night and I'd taken 'im another bottle of whisky sir so 'e might 'ave been very sound asleep. If you woke 'im when he was drunk as all that he'd turn nasty and sack yer on the spot that he would. So I was careful in case he'd think 'e'd told me to see 'im to bed or somethink. He was like that."

"I see. He was a confirmed drunkard was he?"

"Afraid so sir. But otherwise a good master. We've all got our faults, sir."

"Quite. Did he get violent when drunk?"

"Sometimes, sir: it used to take 'im all manner of ways."

"Has he ever had an accident when drunk and hurt himself or anything?"

"Not to my knowledge, sir."

"How long have you been in his service?"

"Ten years, sir."

"Had he ever spoken of suicide in your presence?"

"I've once or twice overheard 'im tell Miss Elsie as 'e would kill hisself if she wouldn't marry 'im. Sir Charles was dead nuts on 'er."

"You have known him for a long time you say: do you think from your knowledge of his character that the trouble last night would overbalance him sufficiently to make him carry out his threat of suicide?"

Corbin considered for a while and then answered, "I shouldn't like to say, sir."

"Did he seem badly upset?"

"Not after the row was over, sir: he seemed as if he'd 'ad the wind taken out of his sails."

"Did he mention suicide to you in the library before you left him for the night?"

"No, sir. He hardly talked at all. He was very quiet and dignified."

"Did you see or hear anything of the quarrel in the lounge beyond the fight you mentioned?"

"Yessir. I was there all the time."

"There all the time?"

"You see what kind of man Sir Charles was," broke in Elsie, "he insisted that the whole quarrel should take place in the butler's presence."

"Did he indeed?" said Richardson. Then to Corbin: "So you saw it all did you?"

"Yessir."

"And you've heard the account I have had of it?"

"Yessir."

"Has any detail been overlooked that might have some bearing on Sir Charles Dorsay's death?"

John was on his feet in an instant. "This is an insult, Inspector," he began. But Richardson cut him short.

"No offence, Mr. Tarren," he snapped, "but I just want to make sure. Now Corbin think very carefully."

Corbin did, and the result of his mental efforts was as follows;

"There is one thing you should know of, sir," said he, slowly, and thoughtfully, "though I hardly like to repeat it, seein' who it concerns, and that is that Miss Elsie told Sir Charles she wished he was dead . . ."

"That's a lie, Corbin," burst out Elsie indignantly, "I did not."

"Well, Miss," stammered the butler, a little abashed, "It was something of that sort—only put in . . ."

"What actually did you say?" broke in the detective, "was it anything like that at all?"

"It really can't matter at all," said Elsie. "Sir Charles was too brutal a man to care in the least whatever was said to him, but all I said, in any case, was that I hoped he'd break his heart with rage and jealousy over John and that I hated him."

"Rather harsh words don't you think?"

"Yes I know, but he'd been so beastly to me that I wanted to hurt him if I could. He made my life unbearable—I would have faced anything rather than stay here a minute longer than I had to."

"How did he make your life unbearable?"

"By his horrible love-making as he called it. I was goaded beyond myself. There are some kind of insults that even a modern girl will resent you know. Inspector."

Richardson looked at Elsie searchingly for a while, then: "You hated Dorsay pretty badly then?" he said.

"How could any self-respecting woman do otherwise? He was a disgrace to his title, a disgrace to his position, he was not fit to live . . . he . . ." She burst into tears.

"Elsie . . . Elsie . . ." remonstrated Tarren.

The Detective waited in stony silence until Elsie had calmed down a little, and then he said to her very quietly:

"Just one more question Miss Mervyn—did you see Sir Charles Dorsay alive for the last time when he left you in here to go to the library?"

"Yes—I have not seen him since at all."

"He left us alone in here," broke in Tarren, "we talked together for a few minutes about our future plans, and then I took her to the door of her room, left her there, and went to bed myself."

"Quite so," said Richardson, a little impatiently, then to Elsie—"will you swear you did not leave your room until the butler fetched you this morning?"

"Yes I will," answered Elsie, looking Richardson steadily in the eyes.

"That will do." Richardson turned again to Corbin, who was very disturbed at his slip—intentional though it was— or, to be more accurate, at its consequences.

"You must remember, Corbin," he said, "you are giving evidence of great importance, and be most careful to be quite accurate."

Corbin apologised all round humbly and submissively, and the Inspector turned his attention to the two women servants.

He found, of course, that the kitchenmaid, having been only introduced into the household the day before and that in the evening, had not so much as seen her employer since he interviewed her a few days before she knew she was engaged. She could give no information whatever about anything and was so obviously terrified at being mixed up with a possible murder that he dismissed her as of no consequence at all.

He was not much more fortunate with the housemaid, Mary Pane, whom, it seems, had her day out on the fatal day, and went straight to bed on her return which was long before Dorsay got home. She slept in the most distant quarter of the house, and heard nothing until Corbin told her of the tragedy.

But, in spite of Richardson trying hard to "keep her to the point," she would insist upon giving an unasked opinion of her late master's character in no measured terms, describing him as "an 'orrible brute," and giving details of his little ways which we hardly think it necessary to repeat. She recounted, too, how the new kitchenmaid had been rendered necessary by the old one going home to "tell her father," and expressed the opinion that the outraged parent in question was, doubtless, the person who had "murdered Sir Charles in 'is bed," adding that it was a "judgment upon 'im," and insisting that "no gentleman would be'ave like Sir Charles 'ad to that poor girl"—which we take the liberty of doubting in view of the fact that misdeeds of this sort have been peculiar to gentlemen since the world began.

As it appeared from further questioning of the censorious housemaid that the father of the insulted kitchenmaid lived somewhere in Scotland, and that by courtesy of the local guardians of the poor; and, further, that his injured daughter had only left "Dorsay Hall" the afternoon preceding Sir Charles' death, Richardson did not think it very likely that the tragedy he was investigating was the vengeance of this particular parent—since he could hardly have heard of his child's reason for throwing up her job before about one in the morning at the earliest.

There now remained only the chauffeur, who lived right away from the mansion in the lodge at the entrance-gates, and so, of course, heard nothing of the tragedy until summoned by the police. From him Richardson gathered that the account of Dorsay he had heard from the housemaid was no exaggeration, and learned that the man had driven Sir Charles to Mdlle. Morone's hotel on the fatal evening.

"The boss told me to wait for him," said the man, "and I waited a pretty decent time too. After a while, as there was no sign of the Guv'nor coming out, I thought I'd stretch my legs a bit and have a smoke. So I got out of the car and lighted up my pipe, strolling about meanwhile, and keeping near the hotel door so that I should be ready to drive away the moment I saw Sir Charles coming. The window just over the door was wide open, and it was not long before I could hear that there was a terrific row going on in that room. I heard the boss's voice and I heard a lady's. The lady's voice I knew too. She was a lady Sir Charles was rather intimate with at one time—not so very long ago either—and had dropped. It seemed that she wanted to be taken back."

"Did she get her way?"

"No. Sir Charles said he didn't want her any more, and was a bit cruel too in the way he put it."

"Did she threaten him?"

The man thought for a moment. "Well sir," he said at last, "she spoke French mostly, and I don't know the language, but she was terrible angry. Blimey! She didn't 'alf go on! But I felt downright sorry for her. Then, all of a sudden a funny thing happened. Mr. Corbin, the butler here, rode up on a bicycle, and dashed past me into the hotel. I heard him call out to the Guv'nor "they're at it" or words to that effect, and both Sir Charles and Corbin hurried down to the car. Of course, I jumped into my seat at one, but I saw the lady follow them down and heard her carry on like a mad woman. They jumped into the car, and the master called out to me to drive straight away home as fast as I could. I started up and off we went. When we got here, they both hurried out, and Sir Charles told me hurriedly that he should not want me or want the car any more that night. So I just drove the car into the garage, locked it up, and went off to get some supper and go to bed. Next thing I knew about this was that Sir Charles had been shot dead, and the police wanted to question me. That's all, sir: on my oath, sir!"

"Humph," muttered Richardson to himself, "the plot thickens!" He asked Corbin to explain his presence that night at the hotel which the butler accordingly did—thus throwing additional light upon Sir Charles Dorsay's nature, and, incidentally, his own. Further, he gave greater details concerning Dorsay's relationship with Mdlle. Morone which were illuminating.

Now one might well wonder how it was that Mr. Walter Corbin had failed to give the police further information about Mdlle. Morone before this, since he was so very anxious to find some person other than himself upon whose shoulders to thrust every possible shadow of responsibility in the matter of his master's gruesome end. As a matter of fact he would have done so, only his mind became so utterly confused and muddled under the battery of questioning by a real live Scotland Yard man that he had not thought of Mdlle. Morone at all until the chauffeur was examined by the police. Now that the affair had actually come up Corbin felt a great sense of satisfaction since it seemed to him to lead the scent well away from him once more.

Nor was the butler the only person who felt glad that this information had been forthcoming. His pleasure was shared quite whole-heartedly by Detective-Inspector Richardson, who saw in a cast-off mistress only a mile or so away, a quite probable solution to the problem he had to solve. Still, if she had indeed broken into "Dorsay Hall" through the library windows in the dead of night and murdered its lord and master, it would be very doubtful if she would return to her hotel—an address known to her victim's chauffeur and to his butler, and an address where he had actually visited her the evening of the tragedy, and during which visit she had made her emotional disturbance evident to the two witnesses who would be certain to be questioned by the police.

But, still, she might be there: she might be bright enough to realise that flight was the greatest confession of guilt she could make to the world at large.

Or yet again she might not be guilty at all, and in that case would almost certain to be still there—possibly as yet in total ignorance that Dorsay was dead. And anyhow, guilty or innocent she might certainly prove to be an important witness.

So thought Richardson, and decided that Mdlle. Morone must be brought to "Dorsay Hall" at once if possible. He dispatched Sir Charles' Rolls Royce driven by a plain-clothes man to her hotel, together with Mr. Walter Corbin to act as spokesman, although accompanied by two more plain-clothes men to ensure that he made no attempt to slip away. For, in spite of everything, the Detective was by no means whole-hearted about Corbin, who, truth to tell, was hardly the kind of man one would expect to find occupying the post of butler in an English country house. Still, nor was Sir Charles Dorsay exactly the kind of man one would choose as the master of such an establishment—and like master like servant.

CHAPTER VIII

HAVING DISPATCHED CORBIN on his errand, Richardson decided that his next move must be to take down the doctor's report. So he asked a constable to summon Dr. Grenville Horton from the library where he had been examining the body.

The surgeon in question was a man of wide experience, and had conducted many a post-mortem examination in cases where foul play might be suspected, but his first remark on being brought before the detective was that never before had he seen such a disgusting sight as that which had met his eyes in that macabre room.

He had found it by no means difficult to form an opinion as to the details of Sir Charles' untimely end, and said that death must have occurred roughly about half-past four or a quarter to five in the morning. The gun must have been held right against the face and both triggers had evidently been pulled at once as the two barrels had been fired simultaneously.

"Do you think it a case of suicide?" asked Richardson.

"No," was the reply. "I don't."

"Why?"

"It would hardly have been possible for the dead man to have fired that gun himself with the barrels jammed against his face."

"Well—could it have been done at all?"

The doctor considered for a few seconds. "It could, but only with the very greatest difficulty. I have measured both the arm of the deceased, and the distance from the end of the barrels to the trigger, and, from my results, deduce that it could only just have been managed with a very great effort—even if he had put the end of the gun in his mouth and in this way shortened it. But one can hardly conceive a man killing himself in this way when he could have used a revolver. There are several pistols too, and plenty of ammunition. Had he killed himself he would surely have used one of these."

"Have you any means of telling if the gun was fired with the barrels in the mouth?"

"Yes, although it is a trifle difficult to tell as the greater part of the front of the head has been blown away: still, had the barrels been held in the mouth the whole head might have been destroyed whereas as it is the back is more or less intact."

"So you think the gun was just held against the face?"

"Yes. But in that case I cannot possibly see how the triggers could have been pulled—that is unless it was done by a piece of string or flexible wire passed round the back of the trigger guard so as to reverse the pull."

"Is there anything to suggest that it was actually done that way?"

"The gun has a very elaborate trigger-guard, and certainly lends itself to such a trick, but there is no sign of the piece of string or wire which certainly should be lying near if it had been used."

'Death, of course, was instantaneous?"

"Certainly: he knew nothing after the trigger was pulled—whoever pulled it."

"How do you think the gun was held—directly in front of him?"

"It might have been—there is no way of telling since there is no ordinary bullet-wound, the shot has ripped the flesh in every possible direction: the barrels might have been pointing directly at him or to one side of his face. Not only so, but the man must certainly have been asleep: otherwise would he have kept still long enough for the shot to be fired? In any case there would have been a struggle, and the room shows no sign of any disturbance of this sort."

"You're right there, doctor, if Dorsay had been awake he must have been very drunk to have been shot like that without putting up a fight. So—unless Dorsay actually did commit suicide with the gun by some trick way of firing it like that—it must have been a pretty brutal kind of murder. The murderer must have crept into the library, got the loaded gun from its place in the rack—or loaded it from stolen cartridges taken from the gun-case—and sneaked up to that old fellow who was sleeping at the table, put the barrels against his face and fired."

The doctor nodded.

"Yes, it's a pretty beastly case, Inspector."

Richardson was about to say something when there was a sudden disturbance, and Mdlle. Morone, in a state of the greatest excitement, rushed into the room with Corbin and two plainclothes men at her heels.

"What is this—what?—Oh, Mon Dieu! Mon Dieu! Tell me, tell me that he is not really dead—Charlie—Dieu de Dieu—where is he?"

The detective turned quickly to the excited woman.

"Are you Mdlle. Morone—the . . . er . . . friend . . . of the late Sir Charles Dorsay?"

"You ask me if I am his . . . friend . . . I am more than any friend could have been. I did love him with all my soul . . . all the life and the heart within me . . . and now you tell me that he . . ."

She broke down into a flood of passionate tears, and dropped on to the sofa.

Richardson was a little impatient, although he tried not to show it.

"Please try to calm yourself madam and answer my questions," he said gently. "I am Detective-Inspector Richardson of Scotland Yard, and I am investigating the death of the late Sir Charles Dorsay. He was shot in the night, and the circumstances appear to point to foul play. I understand from the dead man's butler that you were one of the last people who saw Dorsay yesterday, and that you had a bad disagreement. We should like to have every detail you can give us."

Vesta looked up through her tears. She was trembling in every limb.

"Then he is dead—it is no bad dream. Where is he? Where? Take me to him."

"Afraid that is out of the question. It is no fit sight for a woman."

"But I insist on seeing him. I loved him, loved him . . . and I *will* go where he is . . . I will."

"Please understand that you are officially forbidden to go near the body," said Richardson coldly, "and, if as you say the dead man was dear to you, then it is your duty to do everything in your power to help the police to get to the bottom of the case. Now please . . ."

But Vesta was not to be silenced so easily. She sprang to her feet, her eyes blazing with anger.

"Ah, you English, you English, cold-blooded lot that you are. You would try to keep me from the dear dead one I loved even though he was tired of me: you think that his remains would horrify me, hein? you think I could not look upon him without shuddering? I tell you I adored him, and that he would not frighten me. Let me go to him I tell you— you shall let me go to him . . . Charlie . . . Charlie . . ."

So she went on in a wild rush of words and a sad jumble of languages, finally trying to kneel at Richardson's feet. But it was of no use. He was adamant.

"I shall not allow you to see that body, madam," he informed her, "not, that is, until it is ready for burial after the Coroner's inquest to-morrow."

"Not just for one little minute . . . to kiss him one last long good-night?"

"No. It would be useless. You are not aware perhaps that his whole face has been practically blown away with a shot gun."

Vesta gave a piercing scream that tore the nerves of everyone who heard it to pieces. Then she burst into hysterical laughter. The doctor took her in hand and it was some minutes before she could be calmed.

But then it was only to renew her request to see the body, which was again refused, and this time so sternly that she saw it was useless to plead any more.

"Now," said Richardson at last, "You are Mdlle. Morone?"

She nodded miserably.

"And how long have you known the deceased?"

"You mean . . . poor Charlie?"

"Yes. The late Sir Charles Dorsay."

"About a year. We met in Paris, and became friends . . . close, dear friends . . . We had a flat in a suburb there and were happy together for . . . O such a time . . . then he said he must return to England, and, as he still wanted me then, he brought me with him, and gave me a flat in London. But he could not be with me there he said . . . O no . . . it was impossible in England. The English would not understand. So he went off to his great manor house here, and left me behind. But he came to see me . . . sometimes . . . still. And I watch for him . . . always. Then, one day, after a long time . . . he come no more . . . only a hard man who say . . . he is paid to tell me that I must leave the flat and return no more . . . and that Charlie want me no longer. I do not believe him and tell him to go . . . but alas . . . it was all true . . . because . . . Charlie *himself* come and tell me to go. 'Where?' I ask him. 'To the devil if you like,' he answer. Of course there was a big quarrel between us, and I beg him not to send me away. But of what use? He love me no more . . . eh bien . . . it is finished. I go."

She was crying again, but after a while managed to continue.

"I have no money. Not one penny, but he give me some. Still, it is not money I want. It is *him*. So I used it to find him. I got the name of this house where he lived, and I came to the hotel where you send for me. From there I write to him, and call to see him, and be not answered, nor will he see me. So, at last, I get angry, and threaten to tell what we have been to one another; and so he write and say he is coming to see me. Well, last night, in the evening, he come. And I learn why he want me no more. He has fallen in love with his ward. Her name is Elsie, and he is going to marry her. He offer me more money to go away and say nothing about him to anyone. But it is all no good. There is a terrible and angry scene between us and he go away in spite of everything. His butler has come and told him that he is wanted or something, and they hurry away together in his car. I try to follow, but cannot. He wanted me no more and cared nothing at all what I did. I was angry. So angry that I could kill him. And I would far rather kill him, too, than have somebody else have him. But I am weary with everything, and think it better that I die instead at last—when my anger leave me. So I closed the window of my room, and locked the door. Then I turned on the gas stove. But, ah bah—there is no gas. The meter will not give any more unless I put a shilling in the slot. And I—I had not one shilling—only a few pennies, and the cheque Charlie had left me to buy himself from me . . . and that cheque I had torn to pieces before I had stopped being angry. So I was so poor that I could not even die. And I lay on the bed and thought, and thought, until, at last, I went to sleep. When morning came I thought I would try once more to see Charlie, and find the woman he did love and want to marry, and ask her to have pity on me, and then, perhaps, Charlie would come back,—if he knew she did not want him because he had once loved me. But, as I was thinking it all out, there was a ring on my bell, and I was told that the butler here had come to fetch me to where Charlie lived. I was glad I had not a shilling the night before then, and thought that Charlie wanted to see me. My heart was joyful. But, when I got into that car, the other men told me that my Charlie was . . . dead . . . then my heart broke . . ."

She burst into passionate tears once more. Richardson waited until she had exhausted herself, and then handed her a glass of brandy and soda the doctor had mixed for her.

"Drink this," he said, not unkindly, "and try to pull yourself together a little. It is no use giving way like this you know."

Her grief at Dorsay's end was so real and so evident that Richardson almost dismissed from his mind the possibilities of her being the guilty party.

Still, it was just possible that she might be a consummate actress and all this emotion nothing more than a very able display of her professional abilities. He had known a murderess do something of the sort before. But it was not very likely. So it was in quite gentle tones that he said to her:—

"Now Mdlle. Morone, I am quite aware that you have had a very nasty shock, and I sympathise with your grief. I must nevertheless fulfill the forms of law. So just try to think very clearly and answer the questions I put you."

"Ah," she burst out, "you think that I killed him? Well, I might have done last night I was so angry with him: but I got over my anger and so I did not even try. But if you think I kill him, then take me to prison and hang me. What use in my living any more without even the shilling to buy gas to kill myself—and Charlie dead?"

"I have never suggested that you had anything to do with the case," said Richardson, "at least not in that way. But I must know, for form's sake, where you were from the time Dorsay arrived home here—that is exactly 1 A.M. or a few minutes before, to five in the morning, when, we believe, the shot was fired that killed him. Can you tell us?"

Vesta looked at him wearily. "I have told you already," said she, adding tearfully, "please don't worry me with any more of this terrible questioning—it will drive me mad: I am so troubled that I cannot think."

She shut her eyes and leaned back in the couch. Richardson turned quickly to a constable nearby.

"Bates," said he, "just ask Naylor to step this way for a moment."

The policeman nodded and disappeared into the hall, returning in a few seconds with one of the plain-clothes men who had gone with Corbin to fetch her from the hotel.

"You wanted me, sir?"

"Yes," answered Richardson, "did you make enquiries at Mdlle. Morone's hotel as to her movements after Dorsay drove away in his car?"

"Yes sir."

"What did you get from these enquiries?"

The man produced a notebook and read out the following:—

"After the car had vanished the lady seemed terribly upset and rushed back into her room. She did not stay there more than a few seconds, but came out again into the street, rushing away in a fearful state of mind. She did not come back—according to the night porter—until about five in the morning. Then she went straight to her room and was seen no more until we knocked her up to bring her here."

Richardson turned to Vesta.

"What were you doing between the time you ran out of your hotel last night and the time you returned?" he asked a trifle sharply.

"I don't know. I simply remember running about in the dark wanting to die. I felt all hurt inside, and did not look where I was. Then at last I thought I would go back and put on the gas and go to sleep for ever."

"I see." Richardson turned again to Bates.

"How far is Mdlle. Morone's hotel from here?" he asked.

"About a mile, sir."

"Half an hour's walk?"

"Yessir—perhaps a little more."

Richardson looked hard at Vesta as he asked her:—"Will you swear that you did not come here last night or early this morning?"

"Yes—I did not come near here," she answered, and then burst out again—"I know you think I killed poor Charlie— well it was in my heart to do so, and that perhaps is as bad. Take me and hang me!" she repeated again passionately. "I want to live no more."

Richardson grunted. "Don't excite yourself," he said coldly. "We shall come to no wild conclusions. No innocent person will suffer, depend upon that. But, unless you can produce some person who saw you about five this morning —or evidence that you were not near this place at that time, I must ask you to remain here until I give you permission to leave. And please understand," he continued, raising his voice, and looking round the room, "this applies to everyone

here. Nobody is to leave this house without my express permission!"

Vesta shrugged her shoulders.

"I care nothing where I go or what happens," she answered brokenly.

That evening found Detective-Inspector Richardson of Scotland Yard somewhat troubled in his mind. He had worked
like a nigger on the Dorsay case the whole day through, and
got plenty of evidence too. But it was all terribly ambiguous,
and he could not so much as make up his mind as to whether
Sir Charles had met his end by suicide, murder, or accident.
Not only so, but even the doctor had not been able to say
anything that was not so vague as to be almost useless.

If anything Richardson inclined towards the theory of
murder rather than suicide, mainly on account of the very
original way the man had died—surely far too repulsive an
end to be deliberately chosen by a man owning revolvers and
ammunition. And then, again, how had both triggers been
fired at once if they had been discharged by the victim?

But, if someone else had shot Dorsay, who was it?

At first Richardson had strongly suspected Tarren because
of the powerful motive he would have in the matter of the
will, and on account of the quarrel that had occurred so
shortly before the tragedy. But the difficulty here was that
the motive was lessened by Elsie's five thousand pounds,
and the young fellow really did not seem the kind of man
who would hurt a fly. Moreover his horror at the repulsive
sight that had met his eyes when he had conducted the detective to the scene of the disaster, was so real that it spoke
much in favour of his innocence. And Richardson, who had
well over thirty years' experience of crime and criminals,
had not read guilt in the fellow's eyes.

But there remained the fact that John could not prove that
he had not shot his employer, and this, combined with the
fact that he might be a good actor, and so able to feign emotion, still left him hanging midway between the certainty of
innocence and guilt.

Then again there was Vesta Morone. A cast-off mistress, who like Tarren had been one of the last people who had been in contact with the dead man in life, and had been involved in a passionate quarrel with him. She had been missing from her hotel at a time when the evidence seemed to show the murder had been committed and could prove no alibi. And, although it seemed a singularly sickening way for a woman to kill a man she hated, yet Richardson knew, perfectly well, that, goaded by hatred born of thwarted love, a passionate woman is capable of anything.

But there was her grief at his death, and above all her utter resignation to the possibility that she might be hanged for murder. She made no attempt whatever to avoid arrest, and even asked for death.

This seemed to point to innocence again. But still it might be no more than superb acting. She might be brilliant enough to think that the surest way to escape the hangman was to implore him to execute her.

So she—like John Tarren—was suspended midway between condemnation and acquittal in the mind of the detective.

The few other members of the household appeared to have no special reason for murdering Dorsay—with the exception of course of Elsie Mervyn whose position was much the same as that of her lover. So, linking up Elsie with Tarren in his mental group of "probables," Richardson just regarded the others as "possibles" and not very likely ones at that. Corbin he summed up at once as a crook, but also as the kind of crook who thought far too much of his neck to commit murder.

There was, of course, the possibility that nobody inside the house was responsible. The guilty person might have been a total stranger nobody knew about, who had come in through those windows and done the deed. Richardson had provided for this by putting a gang to work outside the house.

But it all came to nothing. No strangers had been seen in the village, and no local seemed to come reasonably into the "no man's land" of suspicion. Not only so, but the only foot-prints found in the grounds were those of a man which were soon identified as having been made by Dorsay himself by comparison with the shoes he wore.

Naturally enough the finger-prints of the entire household were taken. But these also gave no information whatever. The only prints in the library were those of the dead man, and those made by the police themselves.

Even the gun had no finger-prints to show who had fired it, in spite of the fact that it was drenched in blood.

In fact, so difficult did the whole thing seem when re-garded as murder, that Richardson again mentally reviewed the question of suicide.

Here again there was a motive—Elsie's refusal of Dor-say's offer of marriage: the discovery of the love-affair be-tween Elsie and John, and the knowledge that he was power-less to prevent their marriage.

But there was again the question of the possibility of self-murder by both barrels of that gun. It was possible, but only just.

In fact the case dangled between murder and suicide much in the same way as John Tarren and Vesta Morone dangled between guilt and innocence in the Inspector's mind.

There was plenty to point in either direction, and about the same number of difficulties too.

So Richardson waited impatiently for the arrival of Mr. Hampton the solicitor, who appeared to be the only man who knew anything about Dorsay's finances, and so might be able to furnish some information that would just turn the scale.

What, for instance, if the dead man should happen to have been ruined by one of his many betting transactions? The ruin might be recent and so not yet have made itself evident in the household.

And ruin together with disappointed love, and too much drink, would surely make suicide a likely hypothesis.

It was past nine in the evening before Richardson had the satisfaction of seeing Hampton ushered in by Bates who had been allotted the duty of answering the front-door.

Hampton was an old man of something like seventy summers, grey-haired with heavy features and singularly piercing eyes set beneath thick eyebrows, which, despite his years, were still jet-black.

He appeared to be in a state of terrible excitement, and his dark eyes gleamed in their deep orbits as he fixed them upon first one and then the other member of the assembly, and finally let them rest upon Richardson who came forward to meet him as he crossed the lounge. When he was sufficiently close up, the detective noticed that the lawyer's forehead was covered with beads of sweat. His hands were trembling, and his teeth chattering as if with some uncontrollable fear.

He hardly seemed to listen as Richardson introduced himself, and impatiently waved aside his first questions.

"You tell me," he gasped hoarsely, "that my client Sir Charles Dorsay has come to a violent end?"

Richardson nodded, and was about to say something more when the old man went on hurriedly:

"Unless you have definite evidence that he was murdered by somebody, there can be no doubt about his death. He has committed suicide."

"What makes you say that?"

"This. Sir Charles Dorsay was on the brink of ruin. Technically he has been a pauper for nearly a week."

"Did he know it?" was Richardson's first question when he heard this startling piece of information. But Hampton, instead of answering him, rapped out the apparently irrelevant words:

"What is the time—for God's sake what is the time?"

The C.I.D. man looked at the solicitor curiously; wondering what could be the matter with him. The man was shaking all over like an aspen-leaf. But Richardson's reflections were cut dead short by Hampton repeating his question even more urgently.

"For the love of God man tell me the time!"

Richardson glanced at his watch for a second before answering, "Half-past nine: but, really, Mr. Hampton, I don't see what that has to do with the matter in hand."

Hampton seemed a trifle relieved. "God be thanked," he panted, "We have still two and a half hours before us."

"Eh? Two and a half hours before us? What do you mean?"

Hampton fixed his eyes on Richardson's face, and gazed steadily at him for some seconds before replying. He had composed himself somewhat, and seemed to have ceased to fear. All of a sudden he had become strangely impressive.

He was clad entirely in black, and carried a bag which he now set down beside him on the floor. There was just a touch of white about his neck where his stiff collar projected from his long cape, the opening of which revealed the fact that round his neck was a long gold chain from the end of which dangled a large gold crucifix.

He looked in fact far more like a priest than a solicitor, and the words to which he now gave utterance, have certainly never been spoken before or since by a twentieth century limb of the law. In point of fact such a sentence, in all probability has never been heard since the Middle Ages.

"I mean, sir, that before midnight Sir Charles Dorsay's body must be carried to the family vault, and there submitted to the ritual set down in the *Dorsay Manuscript*—the ritual for the slaying of a *vampire.*"

CHAPTER IX

THAT ANY PERSON LIVING in the present generation could seriously believe that the body of a suicide must be pierced through the heart with a wooden stake to prevent its sucking the blood of the living would have seemed out of the question to any one of Hampton's listeners had they not heard his words with their own ears. Even then they could barely credit their senses.

For one second Richardson thought that the solicitor had been drinking, and that his words were the ill-timed joke of a half-drunken man. But this idea was quickly dispelled by the lawyer's manner. There could be no question but that he was in deadly earnest. His face was white and set, and his eyes had in them that peculiar expression which betokens a grim determination to carry through some terrible task for the salvation of mankind at the risk of more than life itself. Swaying slightly he supported himself by holding on to the antique mantelshelf with one hand, while with the other he gripped the crucifix as if in need of spiritual support as well as physical.

The awful words Hampton uttered were followed by a dead silence which lasted for several seconds, during which time everyone present could almost hear the beating of their hearts above the laboured breathing of the old family solicitor.

Then it was broken from outside the house by a sudden rumble of distant thunder.

Elsie gave a little scream, and gripped hold of Tarren who was beside her. He slid a sheltering arm round her waist, and tried hard to appear quite unconcerned. Vesta Morone sat open-mouthed, and wide-eyed—obviously too terrified to move or to utter a sound. Even Richardson blanched a little and bit his lip, although without losing his composure.

If Hampton had spoken those ominous words in broad daylight, on a sunlit day, under a blue sky—or even under any conditions other than those then existing—the matter would have been just a huge joke, and the lawyer would have had his leg pulled most unmercifully by everybody for his superstition and his credulity. But in that majestic old hall, with its suits of mail standing ghost-like in corners: its black-oak panelling: massive antique furniture: great gothic archways: stained-glass windows, and above all its awful silence and comparatively dim light from its ruby-glazed hanging lantern, it was a different matter. Besides, the other side of the library door lay the master of the house, only a few hours dead. And, even under ordinary circumstances, there is something about the near presence of death that awes even the most materialistic. How much more frightening then is the blood drenched and loathsome mass of mortality that lay in that library only a few yards away from the people who one and all knew that he had died by violence, in all probability self-inflicted?

Richardson tried to force a laugh, failed, and took refuge in anger.

"What nonsense is this, Mr. Hampton?" he snapped.

"It is no nonsense, Inspector," replied the solicitor gravely, "it is a grim reality and it must be faced—to-night—*now!*"

"But you are raving," retorted the detective. "Do you actually suggest that we should submit the body of your late client to such a ridiculous indignity because he may have committed suicide?"

"I do."

"Well, sir, let me tell you that the day of such superstitious rubbish is over long ago. Such a thing has not been done for many hundred years and is utterly illegal to-day. As the representative of law and order here, it is my duty to inform you that the body is not to be touched until it is examined by the Coroner to-morrow morning."

"To-morrow will be too late," cried Hampton excitedly, "and it matters nothing how he met his end since he died by violence—if you ignore my warning things will happen in this house before dawn that will re-awaken a curse that has laid dormant for generations."

"Look here, Mr. Hampton," said Richardson sternly, "if you are foolish enough to believe that a dead man can harm anybody you should at least have the sense to keep your ideas to yourself, and not try to inflict them upon other people—do you realise that you are here to give evidence to the police, and not to force your crack-brained notions upon them in this way."

But Hampton was not to be silenced. "Inspector," said he, "you tell me that I am here to give evidence to the police to-night. You are quite right. I am, and I give you formal notice that I have a statement of the greatest importance to make regarding the late Sir Charles Dorsay. Further I desire that it may be taken down. Do you refuse to hear me?"

"Certainly not—but if you think that I am going to listen to talk about the necessity of burying the dead man at the cross-roads with a stake through his middle or rubbish of that sort you're mistaken. If you have anything in the nature of sane evidence that will assist me in clearing up this case please get on with it at once—but otherwise don't waste both my time and your own."

"I will begin immediately," answered Hampton. "How far what I have to say will help you depends entirely upon yourself: but that you do hear it, and at once, is of the most vital importance."

"Fire away then," snapped Richardson, getting out his notebook, and then, as Hampton was about to speak, "one minute please, let's have your name in full, your address, and one or two other details about who and what you are."

"My name is William Hampton."

"Address?"

"I live at 25, Imperial Mansions, Kensington W."

"Office address?"

"No sir—my home address."

"What is your office address?"

"34, Lincolns Inn Fields."

"Thank you. You are the late Sir Charles Dorsay's solicitor?"

"Yes."

"How long has he been a client of yours?"

"His whole life long. I was his father's solicitor as well."

"I see. And you are thoroughly conversant with his financial and private affairs?"

"I know more about the Dorsays than any man living."

"You do do you? And you tell me that he was ruined?"

"On the brink of ruin."

"Did he know this?"

"Yes."

"For how long?"

"Several days."

"Was there no hope of recovery?"

"None at all. He had lost every penny in the world. Had he lived he would have been forced to mortgage this estate of his."

"How did this ruin come about?"

"Partly through recent heavy losses on the turf; and, partly, through a Stock Exchange collapse."

"I suppose he was very badly upset over this collapse."

"Very badly. He was far too proud to say anything to a soul, but when I told him how things stood I read utter despair in his face—and I feared that he might take his own life. How terribly my fears have been realised."

"Humph!"

"And now, sir," continued Hampton, "I beg that you will permit me to make my statement."

"Very well—carry on."

"Before I start," said the old solicitor, "I want a book from the library—a volume which has a vital bearing on what I am about to say. It will be found in the glazed bookcase just inside the door, no doubt, since as long as I can remember it has been kept there. If the key is missing you had better break the glass and get it out."

"What is the title of this book?"

"It is known as the *Dorsay Manuscript*, and is marked with the coat of arms of the family on the side. There is no other title. It is, roughly, quarto in size, and bound in yellowish parchment. It is written throughout by hand. If you will permit me, I will fetch it."

"One of my men will get it," said Richardson. "I have seen this book, and, oddly enough, I saw it gripped in the dead man's hand. It is in a pretty beastly state—all over blood."

Hampton started at the Inspector's words.

"You say that this manuscript book was gripped in Sir Charles' dead hand!" he exclaimed—"are you sure?"

"There was an old book in his hand, yes," answered Richardson: "and it seems to answer the description of the one you want. As to whether it actually is this manuscript you refer to you will see for yourself."

So saying the detective called out "Rowlands!" and a policeman appeared from the library.

"Yessir."

"Bring me the book that was in the grip of the dead man's hand. Hurry up!"

"Yessir."

The man vanished, to re-appear in a few seconds with the book, which he handed to Richardson, who told him to withdraw.

"Is this the book?" asked the detective of Hampton.

"Yes—that is the *Dorsay Manuscript*," answered the solicitor: "and he died gripping it in his hand! Horrible!"

Without more ado Richardson handed the book to the old fellow and told him to proceed at once with his statement.

Hampton took the volume gingerly. It was undoubtedly an ancient tome, bound in what looked rather like pigskin with a crest beautifully drawn on the spine, and on one side. Otherwise there was no mark at all on the cover. It had been well-preserved and was quite without tear or other damage, although one of its covers was splotched with sticky clots of blood which had evidently been splashed on it from the wounds made by the gun which killed its owner, who apparently had it in his hand at the very moment he met his dreadful end. The edges of the pages were quite rough and untrimmed: the leaves of the book being of a kind of ancient vellum which had gone a deep yellow with age.

Hampton opened the book, and everyone present craned their necks forward to catch a glimpse of its contents. The pages, which were roughly quarto in size, were covered over with handwriting in deep brown ink, which had, no doubt, been black at the time it was written.

Hampton turned to the flyleaf on which was inscribed in the same writing the words:

HENRY DORSAY—HIS BOOKE

There followed another drawing of the crest and the date 1542.

"This book," said Hampton, "has been in the Dorsay family since the reign of Henry VIII. It is the journal—or diary—of Sir Henry Dorsay, and it concerns his father, Sir Phillip Dorsay, who was the curse of the family. An account of the way in which he met his end was written in this book by his son—and further writings by later generations of Dorsays follow this ancient account. The last . . ."

"Yes, yes," interrupted Richardson impatiently. "No doubt you are right, and all this may be very interesting to the British Museum, but it cannot have any connection with a day old suicide, and we want . . ."

"I beg," said Hampton impressively, "that you will not interrupt me. The statement I have to make is of very vital importance. And time is getting short."

"Oh, very well," growled Richardson. "I suppose we are pretty certain the case is one of suicide, and, in any event, we can't do any more to-night. The Coroner will be here to-morrow morning, thank the Lord, and take the whole thing out of my hands. Carry on, Mr. Hampton, and I hope your tale will help at the inquest."

Hampton did, and commenced the relation of a history of strange horrors which would have seemed to be incredible but for the undeniable evidence of its authenticity provided by the old manuscript book, to which the lawyer referred from time to time, and passages from which he allowed his listeners to read for themselves at certain points in his narrative.

Everybody present—even the hardboiled Richardson himself—listened rapt with a kind of disgustful fascination to his every word. The only interruption throughout the narration came from the storm without, which came gradually nearer, and nearer, until, at length, it burst overhead with the fury of ten thousand demons. Such a storm had not been experienced for years, people said afterwards. The rapid alternations of prolonged flashes of lightning and deafening claps of thunder were accompanied by a very deluge of rain, which rattled against the windows of the old Manor like the discharge from countless batteries of machine-guns. And, all the while, through the surrounding darkness, the wind screamed and whistled round the house like the breath of an invisible storm-fiend.

"The first half of this book," began Hampton, "is written in Old English characters, and in the archaic phrasing of 1542. I shall not attempt to decipher it in detail as I am thoroughly conversant with its contents which I am about to repeat to you in modern English. But, if any of you desire confirmation of my tale, I will laboriously go through the writing, word by word, to convince you that I have given a faithful account of what was set down in this journal by Sir Henry Dorsay concerning the end of his father Sir Phillip Dorsay.

"Sir Phillip, who built this old Manor on the site of the medieval castle which once stood here, was one of the worst men in history. Not only was he false and treacherous, but there does not appear to have been a single redeeming feature in his character. The man was hated and feared from one end of the countryside to the other alike for his cruelty, injustice, greed, and brutality.

"Lust and liquor were his two ruling passions, and there was not a man among his tenants who did not live in fear that his sweetheart, wife, or daughter, might be the next victim upon whom Sir Phillip Dorsay should cast his drunken eye. The man's wife, of course, was a broken-hearted misery, and did not survive the birth of her child, who afterwards became Sir Henry Dorsay.

"In spite of the terrible example set by his father, who hated him from the moment of his birth, Henry grew up to be a very different man. He was loved by everyone for his gentleness and nobility, and, during his very early manhood, did his very best to influence his sire for good. But quite in vain. Phillip's wickedness seemed to increase as he grew older.

"Finally, matters came to a head when the old man cast eyes on his son's young wife. Of course, when this became known to Henry, there was a dreadful quarrel between the father and son and, it is said, poor Henry was compelled to resort to violence to save his wife's honour.

"But it was useless. He was overpowered by the evil followers of Sir Phillip and imprisoned in one of the dungeons which at that time still existed under the old moat. Nay—still exists to this very day.

"Unable to rescue her husband, and fearful that he might be put to death by his unnatural father, poor Maude Dorsay realised that her only safety lay in flight. She knew that her beloved Henry would sooner perish than have her debase herself to save him, and she realised that to remain unprotected as she was would be merely to invite what her husband most desired her to avoid.

"Once free she thought it quite likely that she might be able to find means to get Henry released as he had many friends outside Dorsay Hall. So, for the moment, pretending that she favoured her father-in-law's advances, she flattered the old man into believing that he had impressed her with his masterful way in removing obstacles from his path.

"He believed he had made a conquest, and so it was quite an easy matter for her to obtain his gracious permission to 'change her dress.'

"She ran to her room, and slipped through the window into the night. In spite of the fact that she had a gigantic task before her—that of climbing down to the ground from the second storey, yet somehow she managed it, although she bruised herself badly in the process.

"But her flight was discovered, and, of course, Phillip and his associates were soon on her track. As she had to run on foot through the night, and they were mounted on horseback, she had little or no chance of escape. She managed, however, by a miracle, to evade her pursuers by doubling on her tracks, and rushing again past the old Manor, took refuge in a nearby Convent.

"But she had been seen by someone on the lookout at 'Dorsay Hall' and, when the hunting-party returned, baffled and enraged, this spy gave information as to where their quarry was to be found. The next day Phillip rode out to the Convent and demanded that they should deliver up the Lady Maude.

"But the Mother Superior refused, and Phillip was ordered never to approach the place again on pain of the curse of Rome.

"But this roysterer cared nothing for the name of Rome, or the name of God, and so it came about that he committed the crime that has handed his name down to posterity as 'The Curse of the Dorsays.'

"He returned to the Manor-House, and, late that night, a cavalcade of armed men headed by Sir Phillip himself, sacked the Convent. Its two hundred nuns were put to the sword if they were old, and to an even worse fate if they happened to be young. If was, of course, a hopelessly uneven battle, and it was not long before it was practically over, and the unprotected women either dead or carried away to their living death by the drunken men.

"But Phillip had not yet found what he wanted—the Lady Maude. He knew that she must be somewhere in the building, and, as most of his followers had searched in vain, he determined that he would look for her himself. But it was quite in vain. She had vanished as if by magic.

"He ransacked the deserted building from cellar to garret, shouting out persuasions and threats for her to come forth. But no voice replied.

"One of his men at this moment rushed up to him with the news that the Convent was in flames, and he was about to rush out to safety, when he caught sight of a white figure flitting along the old stone stairway.

"Forgetting the danger he was in—forgetting everything in his furious determination to capture the trembling Lady Maude, who had been hiding in one of the cells, and had rushed out on hearing that the place was burning, to make one last effort to escape her persecutor—if only to perish in the fire—Sir Phillip brushed the soldier aside and pursued her.

"Fascinated, the man watched the chase. The girl, weak as she was, had, nevertheless, the strength of desperation, and so evaded capture.

"Higher, and higher, up the winding stone stairway she new—Dorsay after her; until, at length, both were lost to sight.

"The soldier, now determined to make his own escape before it was too late, turned and rushed from the Convent.

"What a sight met his eyes when, at last, he had got out of the burning building.

"The Convent was some eight or ten stories in height, and was surmounted by a great stone cross. From every window tongues of flame were projecting amid volumes of black smoke, and the gigantic conflagration lighted up the midnight sky like some blood-red beacon. The roar of the flames was mingled with the falling of great pieces of masonry, the crackling of ancient timber, and the shrieks of such of the nuns as had been left imprisoned in the Convent to burn to death.

"Suddenly a tiny white figure appeared on the sloping roof which the soldier watching below recognised in an instant as the Lady Maude. She was followed closely by what was, obviously, Sir Phillip. He seemed to be gaining on the girl, and, with what seemed a great effort, caught her garment. She struggled free, leaving the thing in his hands, and dashed across the stonework to the cross which she clambered up as though it were indented with steps, and clasped with her arms as though to keep her balance.

"Sir Phillip, who had lost her for a moment, now saw where she was, and rushed after her. Then, as he approached the foot of the emblem, a tongue of flame suddenly leaped up between the man and his prey. He staggered back, lost his footing, and fell backwards. Almost at the same moment the foot of the cross gave way and it went crashing into the incandescent shell of fire below.

"The stone emblem, with its living burden, had been silhouetted against the horizon, like some gigantic crucifix, and had thrown an enlarged shadow on to the ground, for a great distance, around the burning Convent. Strangely enough, this shadow just fell across the spot where 'Dorsay Hall' stood, and, as the cross fell, it seemed to the many watchers who had crowded from their homes the news of the unbelievable outrage that was in progress, as if some mighty unseen hand had seized it by the base, and using it as a weapon had smote the old Manor House with the flat of the symbol of Christianity.

"In fact the peasantry declared that when at last the sun rose on 'Dorsay Hall' it looked quite different. One and all they declared that a curse had fallen upon it.

"And well they might.

"These were troubled times. The Reformation was at its height: the Monasteries were falling one by one, and their wealth restored to the Crown. Protestant feeling ran high in Court circles; and, no doubt, it is for this reason that the horrible crime of the sack of St. Jude's Convent by Sir Phillip Dorsay and his men was, somehow, never brought home to anyone concerned—save, of course, to the man himself who was dashed to pieces. Indeed, it has even been whispered that the hilts of the men's swords were blessed by Protestant extremists before they set out on their vile mission, just as the Roman Catholic persecutors of the Huguenots are said to have blessed the swords of the leaders of the massacre of St. Bartholomew.

"Sir Phillip Dorsay dead, the title, of course, went to his son Henry, who was released from his imprisonment almost immediately after his father had left home to carry out his last crime. An old servant of the family, horrified at the lengths to which his wicked master had seen fit to let his evil nature lead him, had let him out that terrible night.

"Young Sir Henry never got over his beloved wife's dreadful fate, and could never bring himself to mourn over his evil father's death. He had been among the horrified spectators of the Convent fire, and, although he had rushed to the flaming pile, had, obviously, been powerless to do anything more than pray for a miracle—which, unhappily, was not granted. He saw his young wife perish with his own eyes and a deep gloom settled itself upon him for the rest of his days which nothing ever lifted even for a moment.

"When he succeeded to the title and estate things were very different from what they had been when wicked old Sir Phillip was in power. The new baronet spread happiness right through his domains although he himself was utterly miserable.

"But there seemed indeed to be a curse hanging over the old manor since that awful night of massacre. The place was allowed to fall into decay as Sir Henry took no interest in it, and it became one of the most ghostly spots in the country.

"Sir Henry lived the life of a hermit for the first ten years after his succession shut up in his study buried in his books. It was thought for long that with him would die the name of Dorsay.

"Sir Phillip's remains had never been found, and so there was no funeral or rite of any description to note his passage from this world into the next.

"There was nothing beyond a single line in the family Bible:

" 'Sir Phillip Dorsay—slain by the Hand of Almighty God':—and the date.

"Nothing more. The man's memory was a horror to everyone, and his name was never spoken. There can be little doubt but that he was burned to a cinder; and that, if any mortal remnant remained at all, it was buried somewhere among the ruins of the Convent he had destroyed.

"The gutted ruins of St. Jude's Nunnery were left severely alone and nobody would willingly pass the spot after dark. Strange tales went round the village of what came about there at night. It was said that shortly after midnight the Convent bell would toll—like a passing bell for the murdered inmates—and that the screams of the women could be heard, and the glow of the fire seen, by anybody foolhardy enough to look or to listen.

"One sceptic, who volunteered, in his cups, to stand by the ruin right through one night, was found the following day wandering through the countryside a gibbering maniac. Another villager, who happened to pass the place late in the evening, swore that he had seen old Sir Phillip among the ruins, and heard maniacal laughter mingled with crackling timber and women's screams.

"It was not long before these stories reached the ears of Sir Henry Dorsay, who promptly called in a priest and had the ruined Convent sprinkled with Holy Water and a stone cross erected in memory of the Lady Maude right in the centre of the wreckage, which, otherwise, he would not have touched.

"After this the place was quiet by night as well as by day. But it is a strange fact that the sun never shone again on 'Dorsay Hall.'

"It seemed in fact as if the shadow which the consecrated water and the cross had lifted from the site of St. Jude's Convent had fallen upon the home of its destroyer.

"In this manuscript Sir Henry writes that after the ceremony at the ruin he returned to 'Dorsay Hall': and, passing the room that his father had occupied in life, heard strange noises. He opened the door, and, to his horror, saw his sire's headless and armless body walking across the apartment.

"He turned and fled, and that room was never opened again. Subsequently it was walled up: and exactly where it is is not known to-day. But, somewhere, in this old house, is the door and window-less apartment which has remained undisturbed for centuries.

"Sir Henry was horrorstruck by the apparition, and even more so when the Church refused to perform any sanctifying rites in any part of 'Dorsay Hall' with the words:—

" 'The sins of the fathers are visited upon the children to the third and fourth generation . . . We cannot consecrate the home of Sir Phillip Dorsay for three generations.'

"After that Sir Henry writes that after midnight he used to feel that some evil presence was beside him: standing by his chair in his study: seated on his bed when he retired. The beams from a light dispelled this feeling to some extent—but not entirely. Darkness made it unendurable.

"One night, when he was sitting at his desk writing, a draught blew out his light, and he was plunged into total darkness. Not only was he immediately conscious of that damnable presence in the room, but, as his lamp went out, he heard unmistakable demoniac laughter all round the room.

"And there was another thing. Soon he began to feel a strange urge to take his own life: it seemed as if this beastly, unseen, visitor was suggesting to him that he should kill himself. He thought by daylight that this was the beginning of insanity; and by night he was certain that he was absolutely sane, and even more certain that it would not be long before he gave way to the insistence of the spirit visitant and kill himself.

"Finally he sought a remedy in constant companionship. But this was useless, since nobody would stay with him after dusk either for love or for money.

"He was shunned after midnight like a leper.

"Desperate for his life and sanity, Sir Henry determined that marriage was the only way out. He sought the hands of several beautiful women in vain. His 'curse,' as it was called, frightened every woman he came near.

"Finally, however, the unhappy man appealed to a loving and gentle woman, who, although by no means his equal in birth, was, in every other respect, well worthy to be his mate. She pitied his dreadful plight, listened to the whole dreadful story in deep sympathy, and determined to share his unhappy lot.

"She became Lady Dorsay almost at once, and, brave woman that she was, took up her abode at 'Dorsay Hall' with her husband. Her constant companionship no doubt saved Sir Henry's sanity and gave him an interest in life which helped to make his wretched lot a trifle lighter.

But the horrible phenomenon did not cease: it continued: although, strangely enough, Lady Dorsay was quite unconscious of anything beyond a feeling of intense cold. As the time passed, though, she, too, began to hear diabolical laughter with the fall of midnight, and as it drew nearer and nearer to the birth of her child her consciousness of the horror increased.

"Things reached their climax when Sir Henry had to be prevented from stabbing himself by main force: and, on the very night when his son was born. The birth was accompanied by peals of laughter which were heard not only by the mother in her travail, and by Sir Henry himself, but by the entire household and even by those who happened to live nearby.

"The night following the birth of the heir, the bedridden mother found that, after her delivery of the child, she no longer heard the sounds which, during her months of pregnancy, had so alarmed her. Instead the newly-born infant screamed the whole night through unless his cot was surrounded by lighted candles.

"The troubled mother had not been told of her husband's actual attempt at suicide until she had fully recovered her strength. Noble woman that she was she did everything in her power to stand by her husband in his perpetual ordeal. As long as she was near him and the place was brightly illuminated things were comparatively calm—though he would

speak with a shiver about 'voices in his ear—laughter—
urgings to commit unheard of wickedness!'

"Then he would say that he was consumed with thirst—
awful thirst that nothing could satisfy. He soon began to
drink heavily, although his drinking was not the companion-
ate carousing of his father, but the solitary self-poisoning of
a man no one would come near.

"But alcohol did not relieve his craving, and he said that
thirst was driving him mad. The more he drank, the more he
felt he must drink.

"Two years later he was on his death-bed raving with delirium tremens. He had been there only a few hours when his
end came.

"He died on the stroke of midnight to the accompaniment
of peals of dreadful laughter, while a veritable army of owls
and bats screamed and hooted at the doors of the old manor.

"Directly they knew he was dying, every servant rushed
out of the house, and not one could be induced to return until
daylight. Lady Dorsay was left, alone to attempt to comfort
her husband's last moments.

"She continued this manuscript after his death as he had
implored her to do. She has written here that Sir Henry, who
was in life a most devout man, died, nevertheless, with
dreadful oaths and blasphemies on his foaming lips."

The old lawyer turned over the leaves of the old book as he
spoke the last words of his narrative. Everyone was listening
as if spellbound—even Richardson.

When Hampton paused in his story, the detective rapped
out sharply:

"Well—go on—that is not the end surely . . ."

"Indeed it is not," replied Hampton, "though the end is not
far off."

"Carry on then," ordered Richardson.

And Hampton carried on.

"Sir Henry Dorsay," continued Hampton, "was buried in the
family vault, and, after his funeral, 'Dorsay Hall' grew

strangely quiet for a while. Lady Dorsay continued to live there, brokenhearted at her husband's death and living only for the sake of her child, who—although not yet three years old—was now Sir Richard Dorsay.

"She has continued the old manuscript as I said, before, and her contribution is perhaps the most horrible of its catalogue of terrors.

"She records how one night, sleeping in her husband's room without a light, as was her custom after his death, since she had put down his fears and visions to the ravings of a brain unbalanced by suffering and shock at his first wife's fate, she was awakened out of her sleep by the dreadful feeling that somebody was in the room.

"She had no means of getting a light without walking across the room. She got out of bed, and, overmastering her fear, was about to strike a light with her tinder-box, when she heard her child crying in a strangely *muffled* tone of voice in the next room.

"Forgetting everything she rushed into the child's apartment. There a sight met her eyes which made her unable to sleep for the rest of her days.

"The baby baronet's room was lighted by large windows. Through these uncurtained casements the moon was shining sufficiently brightly to make everything there visible.

"Bending over the cot was her husband. *Sir Henry Dorsay*, in his shroud apparently kissing his boy.

"The next minute and the unspeakable truth burst upon the horrified woman, for, as if disturbed by her cry of amazement, the living-dead Sir Henry lifted his head from the child, and looked full at her.

"His face was the face—not of her loved husband and the father of her child—but the well-known features of *Sir Phillip Dorsay*. But the body was not Phillip's which had been short and stout. It was the tall, thin, body of Sir Henry in all but the actual face.

"His lips were parted in a snarl, revealing long white teeth, and thick sensual lips, which were *dripping with blood—the life blood of her child.*

"One thing alone prevented the woman from losing consciousness—the power of mother-love.

"Like a she-tiger she dashed forward to seize the faintly moaning little body from the cot. But she found that she could not move.

"Instinctively her hand went to her breast and in so doing her fingers touched a little gold crucifix that she happened to have hanging round her neck.

"The moment she touched the amulet she found that she was able to move forward. So she seized it and held it forward. At the same moment, with a snarl of fury, the figure over the cot vanished.

"Lady Dorsay seized her child, and rushed with him into her room. She soon had a light and the household was summoned.

"A doctor was called, and he pronounced that save for loss of blood and fright the child was little the worse. He examined two little punctures in the baby's neck and as he did so crossed himself.

"The story soon became public property and the gruesome cry of *Vampire* went round the countryside within six hours of daylight.

"That night the physician who had attended young Sir Richard, and a priest with several men from the village prized open the tomb of the Dorsays.

"There lay *Sir Henry* just as he had been buried. But the body was fresh and rosy without the least signs of decay. The two eye teeth had grown to about double their ordinary length since death.

"It was evident Sir Henry Dorsay had become a vampire after death and had attacked his own son.

"You will say, sir, as representative of the 20th century law that those were unlightened days. But I will show you that the time when things like this were recognised and dealt with in time were wiser times than those we are now living in. Sir Henry Dorsay's body was pierced through the heart; with a sharp stake and the Burial Service read over it afterwards.

"As the last words of the service died away, a voice—the voice beyond question of Sir Henry—was heard to say: *'It is well—he can no longer drag me from my tomb—in pace requiesco'* (Latin for 'I rest in peace').

At the same moment almost there pierced the air a frightful howl of baffled rage and fury, and a bat flew from the vault.

Those present were amazed at these sounds, and wondered what they portended. But they had done their duty. They had destroyed the Vampire. Or so they thought.

"But no sooner had the slaying of the Vampire been achieved than a light appeared in the study at 'Dorsay Hall.' The place became again as it had been during Sir Henry's life. A house of fear.

"Everyone felt it, and noticed the change, but the little baronet was most affected.

"He declared that there was someone always sitting on his bed at night.

"The same old phenomenon. The same ungodly terror. Little Sir Richard used to say—like his father had said before him—that a voice always was urging him to kill himself. And it was not long either before he actually was found attempting to drown himself in a stream one awful night.

"He was rescued in time and brought back by a search party. Never again was he left alone by night or day until he grew to manhood.

"But the dreadful curse clung to him, and the unhappy Sir Richard cut his throat shortly after the birth of his son and heir.

"Again was heard that laughter and again the fearful curse that seemed to have fastened itself to the Dorsays recurred.

"Like his unhappy father had done before him Sir Richard returned from his tomb and, with the face of the accursed Sir Phillip obliterating his own features, sucked his own widow's blood.

"The unhappy lady died from exhaustion and shock the following morning, and had the horror not been witnessed by her mother-in-law, who remembered the unholy past, she would have been thought mad, when she recounted her tale to the doctor.

"Again the vampire-slaying ceremony was gone through, and the second Dorsay pinioned to his resting-place by the stake. His bride whom he had killed was laid beside him, and submitted to a similar rite for it was held, and rightly, that those who die by the bite of a vampire become vampires also after death.

"But yet again the horror came back to 'Dorsay Hall' and the second child-baronet was haunted by urgings to destroy himself.

"The dreadful truth now became evident, and is here in the *Dorsay Manuscript*.

"Sir Phillip Dorsay, having died, as he did, in the hour of his crowning wickedness became accursed: and such accursed people return as *Vampires* after burial.

"But his body had been destroyed by fire, and thus he could not satisfy his craving for living blood after death. But his vampire soul was eternally seeking to find a suitable human body to become incarnated in as a vampire. By the laws of the demon-world this body must be the body of a direct descendant. And so his son Sir Henry had been haunted by his father and urged to slay himself that his body might be a vehicle for his evil father's lust for blood.

"When he died at last he became *possessed* after death, and Sir Phillip used his son's body in place of the body of his own that had been destroyed. That he chose his grandson for his victim was a necessity, for his son's second wife whom he would have preferred was protected by her crucifix from his attacks.

"Happily he was driven off before he could destroy the child. Of course Sir Henry was held to be the Vampire: though this was not the case; and the distracted father, who could not return to earth to interfere with the powers of hell, had uttered the words 'it is well' when he had seen his body destroyed as a vehicle for his vampire-father.

"Foiled, the demon-soul took control of the next in direct line of descent; and he too became possessed after death, only to be freed by the stake.

"And so it went on. At the death of a Dorsay the maniacal laughter of the earth-bound Sir Phillip has always been heard: laughter of horrible rejoicing at a body in which to satisfy his thirst for blood which he could not gratify without one.

"Likewise at the birth of an heir the same laughter—laughter this time of hope that this child may in time become a vehicle for the vampire-ancestor that ever seeks incarnation in the corpse of a descendant.

"For generations every Dorsay at death from any cause has been pierced through the heart with a sharp stake to prevent it being possessed by the soul of Phillip, and used for the work of Hell.

"But it was found very soon that this only brought about that unbearable haunting of the next of kin and the urge to suicide. This could only be thwarted by consecration of 'Dorsay Hall' for then no evil thing could come near, and the earth-bound demon soul of Phillip would be compelled to wait for ever at the family vault in the hope that some body be laid therein and not submitted to the vampire slaying rites.

"This consecration was carried out after the fourth generation from Sir Henry, and so Dorsays since then have not been driven to the madhouse or to death by their own hand by the voice of their accursed ancestor.

"But the consecration remained effective only so long as no Dorsay met his end by violence. Should this come about then the curse would return and old Sir Phillip again take possession of the last heir.

"Through succeeding generations the Dorsays have all died in their beds quite at peace with both God and men.

"But still the age-old ceremony has been carried out on their bodies at the vault to avoid the soul of Phillip taking possession of the corpse—which the consecration of 'Dorsay Hall' could not have prevented.

"So the demon-soul has been foiled for centuries. But it is deathless—and with every generation it grows in strength and in hate and in that awful thirst it cannot quench for want of a body.

"At the birth of an heir and at the death the laughter of hope has been heard—not in this house—but by the grave-side by the tomb of the Dorsays, where Sir Phillip waits till this very day.

"And now, sir, you must see the vital necessity for imme-diate action," said Hampton, mopping the sweat from his brow. "Sir Charles Dorsay has died by violence, of that there is no doubt whatever. It is very likely that he has died by his own hand; that you will admit.

"This violent death has broken the consecration of this old Manor, and it will again become a place accursed. There is no heir—thank God—but tonight at midnight Sir Phillip's soul will return home after countless years of exile. And this house will become inhabitable.

"Unless Sir Charles' body be treated as a vampire *Sir Phillip will enter and the dead man will come from his tomb.* Through him the Demon-vampire of *Sir Phillip Dorsay* will be loosed upon the world to quench a thirst for blood that has raged for hundreds of years unsated.

"And hell will reign once more, the Curse of the Dorsays will have returned. I implore you, be guided by me, and let us carry that body to the family vault before midnight, and drive a sharp stake through its heart.

"Then we will sprinkle holy water over this house of un-told horrors, and all will be well.

"But, if you refuse, God help us all. For all those who are bitten by vampires become vampires also after death. Like-wise all those who come to violent ends tend to become vampires."

"I don't believe it," broke in Richardson, "it's a legend."

"That you will soon find out," answered Hampton, When that unhappy Lady Dorsay, who had been bitten by the vam-pire soul of Phillip in the body of Sir Richard died, there was seen a black cat jumping over her corpse.

"And a black cat jumping over a body is a sign from Heaven that the corpse is one of the Living Dead, and the vampire rites must be observed for the good of mankind."

"The thing is all Tommy Rot," snapped Richardson. "Your tale has been interesting enough—it shows that the Dorsays were all lunatics if it shows nothing else—but the thing is no more than hereditary insanity. Sir Charles Dorsay may have died by his own hand or anyone else's for what I care. He shall lie here to-night to await the Coroner's inquest to-morrow."

Hampton opened his mouth to speak. His words, however, were frozen upon his lips for the door of the library was opened with a suddenness which startled everybody. Elsie screamed: John Tarren gasped, while even Richardson started forward a step or two and stared with horror-struck eyes as one of the constables flung a great black cat into the lounge, and said, as he did so:

"Excuse me, sir, but this cat got into the room somehow or other, and it fair gives us the creeps—playing about all over the place; skipping round like a kid in a nursery, and *jumping right over that body in there*. It gives us the horrors —straight it does!"

Vesta Morone was seen to open her mouth as if to utter a piercing scream. But every sound was drowned by a sudden deafening clap of thunder.

As it rumbled away into silence, Vesta slid from her chair on to the floor.

She had fainted dead away.

CHAPTER X

VESTA MORONE was by no means the only person who was badly affected by the unforgettable incident which closed our last chapter. Elsie Mervyn, too, was terrified. So terrified that she could not even move to go to the unhappy woman's assistance, and John Tarren gripped the arm of the settee upon which he was seated, trembling in every limb in spite of a valiant attempt to overcome a dreadful feeling of helpless terror which seized him by the very marrow of his bones when that great black cat was thrown out into the lounge by the policeman.

There was a terrible and a morbid triumph on the face of William Hampton. He turned to Richardson, who, hard-boiled man as he was, had received something of a shock at this dramatic confirmation of the lawyer's words—or amazingly strange coincidence—as yet his brain would not Work sufficiently quickly to allow him to make up his mind as to which it was more likely to be, and said to him very sternly.

"You see, sir: a warning from the Supreme: heed it before it is too late."

Without answering him, Richardson walked across the lounge, and raised the limp form of Vesta to her feet. He laid the girl on a couch and bathed her brow with his own pocket-handkerchief which he moistened with soda water from a syphon which stood on a side table nearby.

Gradually her eyes opened and became conscious of her surroundings. Richardson mixed her a whisky and soda and insisted that she drank it all.

"You'll be all right now, Mdlle. Morone," said he, and then he turned to Hampton:

"As to you, sir, all I can say is that my opinion of this case is quite unaltered by your statement. I cannot quite understand, though, why you should have found it necessary to repeat such a tale of horrors in front of two women under the existing circumstances. Knowing what your story was you might have asked them to withdraw until it was over. Both of them have had a very nasty shock what with this unexpected death, this damned thunderstorm, and your gruesome legend."

"You mean to tell me," replied Hampton, "that you do not intend to permit the ceremony of slaying the vampire to proceed?"

"Most certainly I do."

"After hearing the facts?"

"If you call them facts."

"And, above all, after receiving such a warning?"

"If you mean after seeing that cat thrown out of the library and call that a warning—my answer is still the same."

"Your conduct then is most reprehensible," said Hampton. "To-night you will find out that my words were profoundly true—and find it out to your everlasting cost. More, others will suffer, and suffer things unheard of."

"Now look here, Mr. Hampton," said Richardson, angrily, "I am sure that you mean well. But, if you are foolish enough to credit an old legend or even an old history,—I am not. I am a practical man and believe nothing of all these wild theories about vampires, and ghosts, and possession, and other rubbish of the Middle Ages. That body in there is no more horrible to me than a carcase hanging up in a butcher's shop. My business is to investigate the circumstances of Dorsay's death, and I have done so to the very best of my ability. To-morrow morning the Coroner will be here and the case will pass out of my hands. There is nothing more that can be done to-night except for everyone concerned to try to get a little rest and so be as fresh as possible for the inquest in the morning."

"Then your last word on the subject is spoken?"

"Yes."

"Then God help all in this accursed house to-night. It is a few minutes after eleven, and my car is waiting to take me back to London. I will bid you goodnight and be on my way.

If either or both of these ladies would care to accompany me, I should be happy to take them away from a dreadful danger. In fact, I should advise everyone here to leave the place before midnight and not return—if they must return at all—until morning. The police will not listen to a grave warning. Let them remain in charge and reap what they have sown without involving other people."

As he finished speaking Hampton turned to leave the room. But Richardson stopped him.

"See here, Mr. Hampton," he said sharply. "As you said, just now, the police are in charge here. Now I—as the representative in authority—absolutely forbid you—or anyone else—to leave this place to-night. You must all stay under this roof until after the inquest."

The solicitor looked horrified. "I would not stay under this roof to-night for fifty thousand pounds," he exclaimed.

"Daresay not," rejoined Richardson, "but you'll stay for all that. If you attempt to leave I shall have you put under arrest."

"Then at least," pleaded the solicitor, "heed my warning. Come, there is nearly an hour before us. You will not doubt my word when you open the Dorsay vault and see lying there all the past generations of the family with stakes through their hearts. Come, before it is too late."

Here Elsie broke in, "Inspector," she said, "don't you think that it would be better to let Mr. Hampton have his way—even if there is nothing in the legend really, it could not do any harm. And I think we should all feel safer somehow."

"Now, my dear Miss Mervyn," said the detective, "there is nothing whatever to be alarmed at. As to the legend, it may be true or it may not. But to me it seems only to point out that the Dorsays have all been madmen since that fellow began to hear the voices in his ears. There could be no truth whatever in the vampire theory. The whole thing was believed in once upon a time, but modern science has swept all that kind of thing away nowadays. You can rest assured that nothing terrible will happen as our friend here would have you believe. There is no such thing as the supernatural. Take that from me, and I am a man nearly old enough to be your father."

"How can you be so sure?" asked Elsie trembling, "especially after that policeman actually saw the cat jumping over the body."

Richardson patted the frightened girl on the shoulder kindly as he replied:

"Don't you worry, Miss Mervyn. That affair of the cat was nothing more than a silly coincidence. I can hardly blame you for feeling scared about it, but there is no need at all for fear. What you need is a night's sleep, and if I were you I should go to bed. Things will seem much better in the morning I can assure you."

"Oh, but I couldn't go to bed with . . . him . . . in there . . . like that . . . who knows . . . suppose . . . ."

She burst into frightened tears, and John put his arm round her comfortingly.

"Elsie darling, don't . . . don't . . . you will make yourself so ill. I feel sure that Inspector Richardson is right."

"Depend upon it, I am," said the Inspector heartily, "I have seen hundreds of murders, suicides, and crime and criminals of every description, and I have always found that the sane and rational is the right solution to every mystery. You can go to bed, Miss Mervyn, and sleep in peace as undisturbed as if there had been no tragedy in this house at all. I shall stay here all the night through with two able-bodied policeman, all of us armed to the teeth. We shall be within call all night, and I pledge you my word we will protect you from any possible harm."

Elsie tried to smile bravely, but she felt dreadfully frightened and full of horrible forebodings. She clung to her lover like a terrified child.

"I am terrified . . . terrified . . ." she moaned. "I just can't sleep by myself to-night."

"Well then," said John, "somebody must sleep with you to keep you company—I am sure you wouldn't mind Mdlle.

Morone being in your room. No doubt she too will want companionship."

"I will, willingly, share her room to-night," said Vesta. "I, too, am shuddering with a horror that I cannot shake off. Ah, but it is terrible . . . it is unholy this thing . . ." She turned impulsively to Richardson. "Why is it that you will not permit the solicitor to do as he say and make all safe for the night?" she asked, "how do you know that there are not things in this world or in some other that we know not of: things which may do us some dreadful harm? Do you not realise that there are more things in heaven and earth than are dreamed of? It is very well for you to say that science has revealed everything . . . science has as yet found nothing of what is the other side of . . . death . . . is that not so . . . hein? Ah, you English . . . you cold-blooded soldiers and shop-keepers that you are . . . you think only of money and of guns . . . and so you laugh at anything that cannot be bought with gold of destroyed by bullets . . . and like the ostrich that buries his head in the sand say . . . 'There is nothing there because I cannot myself see it' . . ."

"My dear lady," said Richardson, "if you talk all night it will not make me believe in ghosts, and bogies, and ghouls, and vampires, and spooks, and all that rot. The only spirits that are not utter bilge are to be found in bottles. If you must cultivate spirits at all, let the black ones alone and cultivate 'Black and White' instead—or, failing that, Mr. Johnny Walker or Old Tom, and if you only take enough of any or all of these you will see anything you want to—and a good few things that you don't bargain for as well."

John Tarren could not help smiling at this, and even Elsie cheered up a trifle. But Vesta Morone remained serious. She said not another word to Richardson though but went up to Elsie.

"Here," said she, taking a gold chain from around her neck and putting it round Elsie's, "on this chain is a little crucifix, and you can wear it through this night of fear. It will protect you from any harm that may come from evil things in the darkness. I do not want it as you do—I do not matter—for, you see, I am not . . . good . . . as you are . . . and it would protect you better than it would me since you are the more worthy to wear it . . . take it . . . and then you will not need anybody by you to-night . . . as for me . . . I fear nothing for myself . . . I will stay down here and sleep on that couch . . . and what will happen to me will happen . . . what is to be will be . . . you see I am not afraid because I love Charlie . . . alive or dead . . . good or bad . . . and if he did suck my blood . . . what matter for it is his . . . even if he should take me away to hell with him it is only that what I should wish . . ."

Elsie allowed the poor soul to hang the chain round her neck in silence, and then put her arms round her shoulders.

"It is dear of you," she said, "but if you wouldn't mind being beside me to-night I should feel better for a companion."

"And you do not think me not fit to be beside you?"

Elsie was far too scared to worry her head about trifles, and implored the Frenchwoman to share her room. After a little hesitation, she consented; and the two women went upstairs together: although, on Elsie's part at least, most unwillingly.

Richardson saw them go with satisfaction, and, turning to Hampton, who all this while had been sitting in stolid silence clutching his huge crucifix like a drowning man does a life-belt, and staring with bulging eyes at the library door, said: "Now, Mr. Hampton, the ladies have gone to bed, and if they have a bad night you will be mostly to blame. I should advise you to follow their example. There will be a lot to be done in the morning as the whole of Dorsay's papers will have to be gone through and his estate wound up and put in order if there is anything left to set to rights which you would have me doubt. This with the inquest on top of it will mean a busy day for all concerned and for you and me especially."

The lawyer rose to his feet. His face was deathly white with an unnatural, toad-like pallor, and his legs were shaking under him. His eyes were fixed on that fatal door, and, as a distant clock chimed, he counted the strokes aloud in a voice that sounded like the panting of a dying man.

It was eleven-thirty.

"In God's name," he gasped hoarsely, "let me get out of this house before midnight—or let me . . .

"Go to bed, man, and don't be a fool," ordered the detective. The thunderstorm had never stopped for an instant, and raged with extraordinary fury round "Dorsay Hall."

"Listen to that storm," wheezed Hampton, "listen to it . . . My God!"

"What of it?" rejoined the Inspector coldly; "clear the air very nicely, and we shall have cooler weather. The rain'll do good too."

He was making notes as he spoke, seeming barely to notice the shaking man at his side.

"I am terrified . . . terrified . . ." gasped Hampton. "Have you no humanity that you can keep an old man here to-night who implores you to let him go to safety? I undertake that I will return here for the inquest to-morrow—if—Oh God,"—and his teeth rattled—"there ever is an inquest. I will be here as soon as you like after cock crow. But let me go away now . . . anywhere . . . but let me go . . ."

"Even if I did," rejoined Richardson, "you'd never drive to town in this storm . . . you'd be struck by lightning before you'd gone a mile. That would be inhuman if you like to send you out into this tempest. No, sir, you must remain here. And for your own sake I advise you as a friend to get all these morbid fancies out of your head or you'll end up in an asylum."

"Before morning," said the white-haired old man impressively, fixing his terrified blood-shot eyes upon Richardson's face, and raising one shaking hand, "there will be only dead men and maniacs in this house. God help us all . . ." he kept moaning, "God help us!"

Richardson was thoroughly annoyed. "For Heaven's sake drop this impious talk, Mr. Hampton," he said. "It is incredible that you, a man of education and years and experience, should go on like an hysterical woman. Now then, see here—I instruct you to get to bed immediately or I shall put you under arrest as a man out of his senses."

Hampton tried further argument, pleading, and even prayer, but without avail. Richardson was like stone and would not hear him.

So at last he shuffled up to bed with the help of Tarren who felt really sorry for the poor weak old man who was obviously sincerely terrified out of his wits.

"You might have let him go home," said John to Richardson when he came downstairs again, "the poor old boy is nearly crazy with terror."

"I know, I know," snapped the detective irritably. "He ought to be put into a home. He's potty."

"But why couldn't you let the poor old bean get away from here?" asked John again. "He could have had nothing to do with Sir Charles' end."

"No one said he had," rejoined the Inspector, snapping the covers of his notebook together, "but, apart from this damned thunderstorm through which nobody could get a car along, I simply could not let anybody out of the place until the Coroner takes charge to-morrow and I am relieved by another Scotland Yard man. We must keep everybody—innocent or otherwise—in sight until some sort of verdict is arrived at. And candidly, Mr. Tarren, the whole thing's a mess up to now. I think that the man did himself in myself—no doubt he was mad like all his forefathers. Damn good job he leaves no children: people like that are best allowed to die out. Blasted maniacs!"

These words were barely out of Richardson's mouth when there was a fearful crash from the library impossible to describe.

John jumped almost out of his skin. "What's that?" he cried.

Richardson drew a revolver from his pocket and strode to the library door and flung it open.

"What the hell is that blasted row about?" he shouted.

A policeman appeared.

"The french windows have been shattered by a thunderbolt or something, sir," he said—"wind blowing into the room like old Harry."

"Better nail a tarpaulin over the place for tonight," said Richardson, "and get to it quickly, Bates."

"Very good, sir," and the policeman disappeared into the room.

Richardson shut the door and shrugged his shoulders.

"This case tears one's nerves up," he declared, as he mixed himself a strong whisky and drank it down.

Elsie, wrapped in a dressing-gown, now appeared, white to the lips.

"What was that?—Oh, what was that?"

Tarren ran to her and put his arms round her. "It was nothing, darling: only the storm—the library windows have been shattered. You had better go back to bed."

"I can't, John . . . I'm frightened . . . listen . . . what's that?"

There came a sound of regular hammering from the library.

"Only mending the window, dearest—nailing a tarpaulin over the broken frame," said John. "It sounded like . . . just . . . like . . ."

"What, dear?"

"Knocking nails into a coffin . . . Oh! John . . . I'm . . . terrified!"

Tarren took the trembling girl into his arms. They were alone as Richardson had strode out to the hall to speak to the constable on guard there. He pressed his lips on to the white mouth and felt it quivering beneath his kiss. He gathered the shaking form close to him, and all but wrapped her up in his embrace.

"Don't be frightened, my darling," he whispered, "I am here to protect you from every harm. I defy the powers of darkness to take you from me. You are mine, and I will guard you with my very life and soul."

Elsie was a little comforted at the confidence of his words. But it was difficult to shake off her utter terror.

"Are you certain, John," she asked, "that there is no truth in that awful story Mr. Hampton told us to-night?"

"Quite certain, dearest," was the comforting reply. "No doubt the Inspector is right when he says that it proves nothing save that the Dorsays were all mad."

There was a crashing peal of thunder and Elsie screamed. "Hark!—"

"It's only the thunder, dear," said her lover, "you are tired out. Better let me take you back to your room."

Elsie shuddered. "Don't leave me, John . . . Don't leave me or I shall go mad . . . I shall really!"

"No, dearest, you won't," he replied tenderly, "be your own brave self and go to sleep. You have that crucifix round your neck, and you know that even if all these dreadful legends were truth, they all insist that the cross would protect anybody wearing it from the forces of evil. So what have you to fear? Besides you will not be alone. Mdlle. Morone is in your room. She is all alone now too, and you would not like to leave her by herself in this storm, would you?"

"Mdlle. Morone is fast asleep," rejoined Elsie, "nothing seems to disturb her. Yet she seemed to believe that what Mr. Hampton said was true."

"Which, only shows how brave she is," replied John, "come, my sweet. I will take you to your door, and my room is not far off. I am going to bed myself in a few minutes and I shall not take my clothes off: so I shall be within call all night. You must get some rest, sweetheart, and we will be up early in the morning for the inquest. After that all will be over and we can settle down to live happily ever after."

He kissed his sweetheart again and again, and she allowed herself to be taken back to her room.

John left her at the door, which he heard her lock from the inside, and then returned to the lounge where he found Richardson smoking his pipe and meditating.

The Inspector looked up as John entered the lounge.

"Miss Mervyn gone to bed?"

"Yes—poor child, she is so frightened."

"Can't blame her—enough to drive a girl daffy."

"Well, Inspector," said Tarren, "I think I will go to bed too."

"Very wise of you. Good night."

"What about you?"

"I shall stay down here all night: I may sleep if I feel like it, but I shan't take my clothes off. I can't sleep until I've seen the Coroner. And then there may be more in this case than meets the eye. Anyhow, I can sleep down here as well as I could anywhere else. I'm a rational man, thank heaven, and a dead body is just cold meat—and bread and butter—to me."

John shuddered in spite of himself at Richardson's hard common sense, and inwardly envied him. Personally, the young fellow, although by no means sentimentally affected by his hated employer's horrible end, was not used to seeing rooms smothered in blood and fragments of flesh, and the sight had sickened him more than he was prepared to admit—even to himself. And then the added horror of the affair and the supernatural element that Hampton had introduced into it all got on his already jaded nerves and upset him pretty badly. While he did not actually believe in the vampire story, yet he could not bring himself to put the matter out of his mind as rubbish as the detective had boasted of doing. Had Tarren been appealed to, he would without much hesitation have been thankful to leave "Dorsay Hall" as Hampton had implored, and even to have gone so far as to have permitted the stake to have been driven through the dead man for the sake of making assurance doubly sure. But, as he had not the authority to give instructions in the matter, and would not lower his manly dignity to appeal to Richardson who had, of course, he had to accept things as they were.

So he simply bade the Inspector good night and went up to his room.

Richardson had told the servants through the mouth of Corbin that they could go to bed, and said that he would see to it that the place was locked up.

So he pretty well had the house to himself with only the two constables. The dead body had been laid on the table and covered with a sheet. He had inspected the damaged windows and seen to it that the tarpaulin had been properly fixed over the shattered glass and woodwork.

He was pretty satisfied in his mind that the case was one of suicide and that the dead man and his ancestors had been lunatics. But he still had a faint, lingering doubt as to the sincerity of Hampton. It might be possible that the man had brought up this vampire scare just to frighten the police and the others out of the house for some reason of his own. He had examined the *Dorsay Manuscript,* and it looked genuine enough to him. But he reserved his final judgment until an expert could confirm his impression. Further, he wanted conclusive proof of Hampton's tale of Dorsay's financial ruin.

All this would be thrashed out at the inquest. Meanwhile he must be prepared for anything—but it was from this world, and not from the next, that the Inspector thought any manifestations would arise—if any did at all.

As to his personal attitude about the vampire scare, it was, pretty well, as he had represented it to everybody. But, although he would not have cared to admit it, Richardson was by no means as hardboiled as he made out. He was rational enough and hard enough and had little faith in things not of this earth.

But it is one thing to declare, in the presence of people under one's orders, that horrors relating to the great unknown on the other side of the grave are "bosh," and quite another to sit on a couch alone in the dead of night with a body nearby—especially when that body happens to be the remains of a man of evil life and of one who had died a violent and loathsome death, how, it was not altogether clear. And worse still when the body is the corpse of the last of an accursed race, and a coincidence—if it *was* a coincidence— had volunteered confirmation of the worst . . .

Black cats did not usually make a practice of jumping over dead bodies. And there it was in the manuscript in black and white—"He over whom a black cat doth jump after death—that man is a man accursed—even a vampire!—Be

warned then and drive a stake through his heart, ere the unholy befall mankind therefore."

It is very well to say that science has swept away all these
hidden things our forefathers believed in. But has it?

Well—perhaps—in a sense.

But it has also taught us to believe in other things which it
has proved to be facts: things which would have sent us to
the stake a few hundred years ago to burn as wizards who
knew too much.

Furthermore, science is only the rediscovery of forgotten
facts, and, since things always move in circles, why should
not the wheel turn right round and the old spoke come up
again?

And suppose that old spoke happened to be the spoke of
the truth of the existence of *vampires!!!*

Was not the discovery of the value of blood transfusions
in surgery a few years ago just the beginning of something
horribly like this?

All this went through Richardson's mind as he lay back on
the couch turning the case over in his mind.

He put the thoughts angrily away, and gripped the handle
of the automatic pistol in his pocket with which weapon of
modern science he could have riddled a dozen men like
sieves at two hundred yards without reloading.

Like Scrooge in *A Christmas Carol* he uttered the word
"humbug" to himself aloud.

But still the wretched thoughts would return, and he could
not shake them off.

Next he thought that he heard a faint sound from somewhere near.

He was on the alert in a second and listened intently.

He had made no mistake. There *was* a sound somewhere
in that old house.

It was a gentle chuckle: a horrible, hollow, laugh which
swelled out into a peal of hellish merriment, and then died
away.

It needed only this to make up Richardson's mind for him. He would definitely set his mind to rest and lay this bogey for ever. That sound must have been a figment of imagination. He would show himself and everyone else that vampires were only pretty girls and not dead men.

He looked at his watch. It wanted a quarter of an hour to midnight.

There was plenty of time.

He rose from his seat and walked out into the hall where there was a constable on duty.

"All quiet?" he asked.

"All quiet, sir," was the reply.

Richardson returned to the lounge and opened the library door where there was a bright light burning. A policeman sat over the body under the sheet on the writing table.

"Bates," called Richardson softly.

"Sir?"

"I think that there may be an attempt to get at the body tonight, and I want to catch someone red-handed. Now listen to my instructions very carefully."

"Yessir."

"You are to take a dark lantern and your pistol and seat yourself with your back to the french windows there. Be ready for an attempt to enter on the part of someone from outside, and if anyone does come in shoot them and kill them if you like: they'll deserve all they get. Understand?

"Yessir."

Bates took up the position he was told to, and Richardson continued.

"I am going to leave you alone in this room till morning— you don't mind?"

"No, sir."

"Good. Now you are going to be locked in from outside."

"Yessir."

Richardson went to the other constable in the hall. "You, Rowlands, come out with me."

The man obeyed. Richardson locked the library door from outside and gave the key to the constable.

"Put this in your pocket."

"Yessir." And it was done.

"Now seat yourself with your back to the library door, and have your pistol ready. Also have your lantern lighted but the cover closed. Be ready at any moment to flash a light on and fire at anyone who either comes out of the library or tries to get in—understand?"

"Yessir."

"I shall be within call. I have put the library lights out, and I am going to have the lounge dark too. I am going to affect to go to bed. But I shall be armed and ready when you call if you have to. Blow your whistle at any sound or anything you see."

"Very good, sir."

"If anyone tries to get in the house from outside or go into that room they will have no luck," said Richardson.

"No, sir. Good-night, sir."

"Good-night."

The constable was duly settled at his post, and Richardson put out the lights and softly went out into the hall.

Throwing himself on a divan that stood in a corner near the great fireplace he again gave himself to reflection on the case.

If the night passed without event then he would have laid the family ghost forever.

But suppose it didn't?

He addressed himself again more roughly than he had before.

"Humbug!" he growled.

As he finished his mental reproof to his own doubts the old clock chimed into the night . . .

One . . . two . . . three . . . four . . . five . . . six . . . seven . . . eight . . . nine . . . ten . . . eleven . . .

TWELVE!!!

Dead silence—except for the rain, faint thunder in the distance, and a flicker of summer lightning. Richardson yawned, tired out, and dozed off.

CHAPTER XI

THE STORM HAD DIED DOWN CONSIDERABLY, and the old house was mysteriously quiet. So Richardson slept on for some time quite undisturbed. The constant patter of the rain and the periodical rumble of the thunder gradually seemed to the sleeper to recede into the distance, until, at length, he was no longer conscious of any sound whatever.

The couch, upon which he was lying, commanded an excellent view of the lounge which opened out of the old hall, and it was for this reason he had chosen it as his resting-place. The faintest sound from Rowlands—the policeman who was stationed outside the library door—would waken him immediately. So he felt that he could go right off to sleep without taking the least risk of being "caught napping" in the figurative sense of the term.

And, worn out as he was, the man certainly badly needed an hour or two's sleep.

It was not very long, however, before he began to be troubled by horrible dreams; which, in his sub-conscious mind, he put down to a direct reaction from the impressively gruesome tale told by Hampton.

He thought he saw Rowlands fall off his chair sideways, and lie quite still: then he dreamed that, in the lurid light of a prolonged flash of lightning, he saw the library door open and a dark figure, with outstretched arms, creep from the room, and across the lounge towards the great staircase that led from this apartment to the bedrooms. He dreamed that this figure was giggling to itself—sniggering in damnable merriment over that which would make the angels shudder, and provoke laughter in the hells.

Then he dreamed that he arose and followed this unholy figment of sleep: that he followed it right through the back wall of the old Manor House across the grounds and into the burial-ground which adjoined the Parish Church. It led him to a massive tomb of black marble, the great doors of which swung open to admit it, and closed again, with a sickening crash, as soon as he had entered.

And he knew that he was in the ancestral tomb of the Dorsays. He looked round him in awe at the enshrouded figures of the dead which lay on the shelves in their coffins, some of which were comparatively new with gleaming brass handles and inscription-plates and others made of stone and of great age; while others, again, had mouldered away exposing their macabre contents. He saw in disgust that everybody there which could be seen had a wooden stake driven through its breast right into the heavy shelf beneath.

Then, in his dream, he thought that he remembered that in gazing round the tomb he had forgotten that he must follow that mysterious figure which he had come out to track. Of course it was the clue to the mystery of Sir Charles' death.

So he hurried from the vault passing again in his dream through a solid wall, and out into the dismal churchyard. Was he too late? he thought. Had that figure eluded him?

No. There it was flitting through the night, and he dreamed that he hastened after it, following it through long deserted country lanes to a desolate spot where there was a ruin. And the man knew that this ruin must be the ruin of the old Convent mentioned by Hampton in his story.

And then he found himself following the figure up winding stone stairways, and he wondered vaguely in his dream how it was that a ruin could look so solid. But, of course, that only proved that he was dreaming. He must rouse himself and wake up—shake off all this nonsense and relieve one of the constables.

But he found that he could not open his fast-closed eyes: although the fact of their being closed did not prevent his seeing clearly. Another funny thing about dreaming.

And then again he remembered that he must keep on the track of the figure that had led him out, and in his dreaming hurried along ever more quickly. It led him ever higher and higher right on to a stone plateau—the roof of some lofty building or other.

There was the figure he was after—and sure enough, too, there was a second figure which the first apparently had been pursuing.

He ran after it helter-skelter through the night: at all costs he must overtake the key to the mystery; and, besides, there was now this woman to be considered. He dreamed that he drew his pistol and called to the man to stop but in vain.

On, on, through the chill night air, across the roof, dashed the man: ever gaining ground on the woman, and leaving Richardson in the distance running after it until he felt his heart would burst. Then, suddenly, he heard the woman scream out, and he knew in his sleep that *it* had caught her. There, too, was the figure just in front of him—one final effort and he would be able to seize it, and, perhaps, rescue the woman.

So he leapt into the blackness before him. As he did so he realised, in one dreadful moment, that his quarry had tricked him. He had stepped over the edge of the roof of the lofty Convent and was falling . . . down . . . down . . . down . . . with the woman's piercing screams and the sound of hellish laughter in his ears.

Down . . . Down . . . *down* . . . Crash!!!

Richardson awoke with a violent start in a cold sweat. How long he had been asleep and dreaming all these evil things he could not imagine. That he was awake now he did not doubt. He was lying on his couch in the hall his eyes wide open and every sense alert. He had been awakened with a deafening clap of thunder. Or so he thought for a second or two. Then, in an instant, when the thunder had died down and other sounds become audible, he realised the dreadful truth.

A woman's piercing screams were ringing through the house: the shrieks he had heard in his dream had been genuine screams—and the real cause of his having awakened so suddenly.

Above the screams he heard a confused noise of shouting. There was old William Hampton calling out—"The Curse— God in Heaven—the Curse!" and John Tarren's voice yelling out his own name:—

"Richardson! Damn you, answer me! Richardson! *Richardson!!*"

He sprang to his feet, and, without attempting to find the electric light switches, flashed on his pocket torch and rushed upstairs.

On the landing, which was flooded with light from the chandelier, was John Tarren, battering at one of the bedroom doors with his bare hands, from behind which were issuing the screams Richardson had heard.

Hampton, fully dressed, was standing nearby. The sweat was streaming from his forehead, the veins of which were swollen to bursting-point. The old man was babbling like an hysterical child, and had, obviously, lost his senses. Corbin and the two maidservants were standing by huddled together in a confused heap on a great oaken chest.

"Get that door down—get it open I tell you! Elsie's locked herself in there, and God above knows what's happening to her!" screamed Tarren. "Get that damned door open!"

Richardson hurled his weight against it, but in vain: the door was far too massively built to give way so easily. A second time the detective tried: this time with John's help. But the door would not yield. It was built of that iron-like oak, and could withstand almost any shock.

There was only one thing to be done, and Richardson did it. He shouted to Elsie to stand clear of the door, and right to one side, and blew in the comparatively modern lock with his revolver. This proved effective, and the detective rushed into the bedroom followed by John, Corbin, and the still babbling Hampton.

Elsie had fainted, and was lying in a heap in one corner of the apartment in her nightdress. The window was wide open and the curtains blowing inwards with the wind and the pelting rain. The electric fitting was lighted and blowing to and fro in the draught from the window.

John dashed to Elsie and picked her up bodily in his arms, carrying her out to the landing where he laid her on the oaken chest and did all he could to restore her. One of the maids had a smelling-bottle, and this revived the girl a little.

"What happened? My darling, tell me what happened?" asked John as Elsie opened her eyes after what seemed to him an eternity.

"Oh, John, dearest," she replied in a hoarse whisper he could barely recognise as her voice, "John, dearest . . ."

"What is it, my darling? Tell me—I beg you tell me?"

"I have seen something terrible, John . . . and I don't think I shall ever sleep any more."

"What is it, my sweetheart?"

"Something woke me up, John . . . I did not know what it was until there was a flash of lightning . . . and then . . . then . . . I saw someone . . . a man . . . bending over the bed . . . over Vesta Morone it was . . . I tried to move; but, somehow, I was too terrified and I just daren't . . . then . . . I screamed out and screamed . . . I couldn't help myself . . . and, whatever . . . *that* was, it rushed across the room and out of the window I think . . . but it was too dark to see really where it went . . . I got out of bed somehow and found the switch, and, when I put the light on, I saw there was . . . blood on the bed . . . and I sort of lost hold of myself . . . I don't remember anything more . . ."

"Can't you tell me who it was you saw?"

"It . . . looked . . . like . . . *Sir Charles* . . ."

"It couldn't have been."

"I know it was . . . I know it was . . . Oh, John, help me or I shall go mad, . . . and I'd be so frightened to go mad . . . don't let me . . . Oh, John, darling . . . don't let me . . ."

Tarren gasped. Could the seemingly impossible have actually happened?

Hampton had been listening to Elsie as if the fate of the world depended upon her every word. At her last hysterical declaration his eyes seemed to bulge forward right out of their sockets like bloodshot balls of tortured fire. He burst into maniacal laughter and before anybody could stop him drew a pocket revolver and shot himself dead.

Meanwhile Richardson in the bedroom had gone across to the great four-poster bed on which lay the huddled form of Vesta Morone. He touched her, and realised to his horror that she was dead and nearly cold.

Worse still, further examination showed that there were two little blood-clotted punctures in her throat. And the carpet bore unmistakable muddy footmarks. Someone had certainly been in that room.

What had happened?

The report of Hampton's pistol brought the detective out on to the landing. Tarren and Corbin had both the same tale to tell. Hampton had taken his own life in a moment of utter insanity through utter fear.

The suicide, coming on top of the horrors of the night, had all but unbalanced Elsie who had again sunk into a merciful unconsciousness.

After one comprehensive glance at the dead lawyer, Richardson ran downstairs again to summon one of the constables. He could hardly understand their inhuman tenacity to their posts through all that had happened.

Surely one of them had heard it all. When he got to the lounge he shouted the name of the policeman whom he had posted outside the library door. But there was no answer.

Full of confusion Richardson fumbled about until he found the switches: and when, at last, he got the electric light on, he saw, to his horror, that Rowlands had not answered him for the good reason that he had fallen from his chair, and was lying on his side on the ground.

Not only so, but the library door was wide open! And he had locked it.

He bent over the constable for a second. There was no doubt whatever about it. The man was dead.

But what, in Heaven's name, had killed him?

The detective stepped over the limp figure and hurried into the library, gripping his pistol as he did so. He switched on the light which he had left burning when he locked the room and someone had apparently turned off.

Never, in the whole of his afterlife, did he forget the sight that met his eyes when he entered that room.

The tarpaulin, which he had had nailed over the french windows had been ripped open, as if with a knife, and the storm was blowing furiously in through the jagged tear.

Bates, the constable, who had been stationed inside the window had completely disappeared. The man's helmet lay beside his overturned chair beside his still fully loaded pistol.

The sheet which had covered the mortal remnants of Sir Charles Dorsay lay in a heap near the table on which the corpse had been laid out for the inquest.

But the body itself was—GONE!!!

CHAPTER XII

FOR ONE DREADFUL MOMENT Detective-Inspector Richardson knew the meaning of fear: fear in the worst possible form in which it can assail a human being: the unutterable dread of the unknown beyond the grave which has gripped the imagination of men of all races, and in all ages, and filled more madhouses than anything else in the world.

Fully two minutes he stood there gazing open-mouthed at the empty writing-table—hardly able to credit his senses. There was no doubt about it. The body of Sir Charles Dorsay had vanished from within a locked room. The armed constable guarding the door was stone dead, and the policeman who had stood sentinel over the body had disappeared, and the fact that his loaded pistol and helmet were lying on the ground there seemed to point to flight.

What had Bates seen in that library? Had he indeed deserted his post and run away—or was he perchance lying dead somewhere, like his unfortunate colleague Rowlands?

Richardson shuddered and pulling himself together with an effort peered out through the french windows thinking he might see Bates lying somewhere out there.

But there was no sign of the man. The grounds were quite deserted, and not a soul in sight. In the wet mud, however, the experienced eye of the detective read something of the solution to the mystery of the man's disappearance.

Bates' footprints—or what were in all probability his footprints—led from the french windows into the grounds, disappearing into the far distance. And examination showed the detective that they had been made by a man running for his life—since the marks were made by the toes of the boots alone.

The trail ended at a side wall: the policeman had evidently climbed over trying to reach safety from something he was fleeing from.

What could it have been?

Richardson examined the lock of the library door. It was unbroken. The door had been opened with a key. He again bent over the prostrate Rowlands. The library key was still in his pocket where he had put it when it was given to him.

The man's revolver was lying beside him unfired.

Richardson possessed himself of the weapon as he had done in the case of Bates' discarded pistol. He felt that he could not be armed too heavily.

What could be the explanation of what he had seen? Could it really be possible that an undoubtedly dead man had risen up from that table, opened the door from the inside, somehow or other, and killed an able-bodied policeman; and then climbed into a bedroom window and murdered a woman—apparently by sucking her blood?

It seemed an absurd hypothesis, but what other explanation was there? A glance at the dead constable's throat confirmed the worst. *There were two little gashes in the man's throat from which a clotted trickle of blood had dribbled down on to the floor.* He had died in the same way as Vesta Morone!

Cold shivers ran down Richardson's spine. He remembered the first part of his dream: how he had seen the policeman fall over from his chair and that horrible figure come from the library. What could be the explanation of this coincidence between dream and fact? He had seen the man fall in his dream and he *had* fallen; he had seen the library door open in his dream and it *had* been opened: was it not likely then—vilely likely—that someone had come out of that room just as he had dreamed?

But, if so, God help his own sanity, and that of the civilised world.

Then, suddenly, he thought of a possible solution: it was only the most slender of chances that it might be so—yet

Richardson clutched at it as a drowning man will clutch a straw to keep himself from sinking.

Bates, the constable inside the room, had vanished. Suppose he had removed that body and hidden it somewhere and then returned to open that door and kill Rowlands and Vesta Morone. But, in that case, how had he opened the door from inside the room. He must have had a duplicate key.

But if Bates had held a duplicate key of the library and had murdered his fellow-constable and Vesta Morone, how had he got hold of that key, and in what way had he killed his victims?

Those little gashes in the throats of the bodies would not have caused death—unless they had been the gateways through which the victim's life-blood had been sucked out.

And why had Bates done this thing—if he had done it?

It would point to one thing only—and that thing was this:—Bates must be the person involved in the death of Sir Charles Dorsay.

Richardson thought over the possibility and remembered that Bates was a local man. He had been attached to the police-station in that village for some fifteen years.

This made the idea of the man being involved seem more possible than before.

But there were difficulties—motive?—means of killing Vesta and Rowlands. And why had he killed the Frenchwoman?

"She must have known too much," thought Richardson to himself. "Bates must be the key to the mystery: any other solution is impossible."

This thought was comforting to a degree. But still his powers of reasoning told him that in any other circumstances he would have dismissed the idea of the constable being concerned in the matter as absurd.

It was only the fearful alternative—the alternative which would establish a horrible superstition as a fact that made him cling to the explanation which seemed more reasonable.

He cursed himself for a fool for giving a local man a post of trust instead of using a Scotland Yard man. Why had he let Bates relieve a London policeman?

Richardson rushed upstairs again immediately he had regained control of himself once more in the manner we have detailed above.

John had taken the collapsed Elsie into another bedroom where with the assistance of Mary Pane, the housemaid, attempts were being made to restore her.

Richardson, with the assistance of Corbin, moved the body of Hampton into the room where Vesta Morone was lying in her last sleep. He covered the body up and joined Tarren.

He was in the midst of telling John what he had found downstairs and setting forth the explanation of the mystery he had formed in his mind when two things happened.

The first was that Elsie opened her eyes again unseen by both of the men and listened in mute terror to what he was saying: the other was that there suddenly came an almighty hammering and banging at the hall door.

"What's that?—what's that?" screamed Elsie.

Both John and Richardson had been startled out of their wits by this mad knocking which got more urgent every moment. It seemed as if someone was trying to batter the door down.

Corbin came rushing into the room wild-eyed.

"Listen to that knocking," he gasped, "who is it—who in God's name is it—I can't stand it sir . . . I . . . ."

"I'd better go and open the door," said the detective, but, in his heart of hearts, he felt like anything but going downstairs to open that door and let in whoever it was demanding admission so violently.

"Don't go—don't, don't," begged Elsie . . .

"I must go," was Richardson's answer.

"Oh no, no, no . . . ." shrieked the girl, beside herself with fear . . .

"Come on, Tarren," said the Inspector, handing John one of the three revolvers. He turned to Corbin, and rapped out: "You had better come too. We might all three have our work cut out."

"Don't leave me—don't leave me!" cried Elsie. "John, don't leave me if you love me ... I shall go mad if you do ..."

She was shaking all over like one with an ague. Her teeth were chattering in her head and her eyes shone with an unnatural lustre born of the most utter terror Richardson had ever seen.

"You had better come along too," he said, with a great and sympathetic understanding in his voice. "We'll look after you."

"But why go to the door?" asked Elsie trembling.

"We must open that door," replied Richardson, "that knocking may be the end of all this damned mystery. Come now, be a brave girl, and either stay up here or if you can't be alone then get on a coat or something and come down."

Elsie made a great effort and Tarren helped her off the bed. She wrapped the quilt round her, and came downstairs with her lover's arm round her.

The knocking continued like the beating of five thousand smiths' hammers, and, led by Richardson, they all went down to the great hall-door.

"For God's sake leave the chain on," whispered John to Richardson, who nodded briefly, and, flooding the hall with light, gripped his pistol in one hand, while, with the other, he commenced unfastening the door.

Thrusting Elsie behind him John also drew his revolver and stood with Corbin, whose weapon was shaking so great was his agitation—the three men making a circle right round the door. They were all ready to open a battery of bullets at any second which could have riddled a small army.

Leaving the heavy chain still on Richardson opened the door a crack, and called out:

"Who is there? What do you want?"

The answer came immediately, and startled the detective so much that he very nearly dropped his automatic.

"Open the door," screamed out a voice like that of a soul in torment. "For the love of God, sir, open the door and let me in—"

Bates, the missing constable, was standing hat-less outside.

"My God—Bates!" shouted Richardson, and dragged the chain off opening the door wide, just as the policeman collapsed on the steps.

He picked up the limp policeman and half dragged half carried him into the lounge.

Corbin again closed and barricaded the front door: then he followed Richardson into the lounge.

John led the terrified Elsie to the couch, while Richardson and Corbin tried to restore Bates.

Huddled together, the two maidservants gazed mute with terror at what was going forward.

It was about five minutes before the constable opened his eyes. Then he gazed wildly about him, gasping for breath. He seemed half-dead. He was bareheaded and covered with mud, as well as soaked through with rain.

"Where have you been?" asked Richardson. "Take it easy now and tell me—why did you leave your post?—what happened man—*what happened?*"

"I left my post ..." gasped Bates "I own it, sir ... I couldn't help it ... I had to ... I ... saw ... *him!*"

"Who did you see?" asked Richardson. Bates was breathing heavily and seemed to have sunk into a kind of stupor. It was only with difficulty that he could be roused.

When at length he could speak again he rasped out:

"I was asleep, sir ... I grew tired of watching in there ... and somehow dropped off ... I didn't mean to ... then something woke me up ... and I saw ... a ... man standing over me ... and ... saw that it was ... *him!*"

"Who?"

"It was the dead man, sir ... Sir Charles ... he must have got up from that table ... he was ... giggling and laughing to himself . . . I've seen Sir Charles in life on and off for fifty years . . . but never with a face on him like that . . . he bent down over me . . . and I turned and ran . . . ran . . . ran . . . He had come back from the dead, sir . . . old Mr. Hampton was quite right, sir . . . we didn't ought to . . . have left . . . that . . . body . . . It was the living dead I saw, sir . . . with my own eyes . . . and I'm done for, sir . . . done for, sir . . . It's . . . blasted . . . my soul . . . sir . . ."

Here Bates collapsed and no effort could rouse him.

Richardson stooped over him and listened to his heart.

It was beating faintly.

The detective poured water on Bates' forehead, and he opened his eyes once more very faintly. He was sinking fast.

"I suppose I must have run round in little circles, sir . . . and I kept on banging into the wall . . . I fell down in a heap at last . . . and . . . I don't remember what happened next . . . but at last I saw a light here, sir . . . and I crawled along till I found myself at the door. And thank God . . . you heard my knocking . . . in time . . ."

Bates' eyes were glazing, and his voice was not above a hoarse whisper . . . suddenly his words ran into each other and became inarticulate drivel . . .

Two minutes later he was dead. His heart had stopped.

Wide-eyed with horror Elsie heard the constable's terrible words, and uttered a piercing scream that echoed and re-echoed throughout the place.

Richardson was at the end of his tether.

Bates' story agreed with his researches. His first theory was true. The constable had run away terrified by what he had seen happen in that room of untold horror.

And he must have seen the body rise from the table.

As Richardson bent over the dead policeman the sound of faint laughter could be heard from somewhere—where God knows.

That fiend-like laughter again.

So, after all, there had been truth in the tale Hampton had told—and a deep wisdom in his insistence that Sir Charles' body should be pierced through the heart with a stake!

Richardson suddenly felt himself gripped with a panic. He was no coward, this detective. He had passed his whole life in criminal detection and had come across many of the most dangerous criminals of his day without knowing what it was to be afraid. He had passed through the Great War without getting a scratch, and had seen men blown to pieces on either side of him without turning a hair. But now he felt that terrible fear that had overcome him when first he saw Dorsay's body had disappeared, return with redoubled force. Elsie grabbed him by the arm. "Quick—quick!" she gasped . . . "Let us get away from here before it is too late . . . this place has a curse on it . . . come . . ."

"Richardson," gasped Tarren, whose eyes were protruding and bloodshot, and whose face was ashen-grey, "for God's sake let us find that body and hammer a stake through its heart. We were damned fools not to heed poor old Hampton's warning."

"No use," snapped Richardson "—it's gone—God knows where, and God knows what has happened."

He turned to Elsie.

"Come," said he hurriedly, "we had better clear out of this place at once—it's unholy . . . the whole thing's beyond me . . . and we'd better get out . . . leave the dead to bury its own dead . . . and save our skins from hell before it's too late . . ."

"Yes," said Elsie, "let's go . . . anywhere . . . the streets rather than this house of death—this house of fear!"

"Come along everyone," said Richardson. "No—stay— I'll phone to the Yard—it won't take a second . . . let them send someone else here . . . I'm done . . ."

The telephone was at his elbow on a side-table. He picked up the receiver and dialed the emergency O.

But there was no reply. The storm must have put the thing out of action. He threw it down with an oath.

"The damned thing's dead," he snapped, "come—"

He had barely uttered these words when the lights all went out.

What exactly happened after that nobody knew. But there was utter chaos and the wildest confusion.

"Put those God-damned lights on," screamed Richardson in hysteria "—put them on, blast you!" He had lost control, and knew not whom he was addressing.

Tarren heard Elsie scream, and shriek out "Help me, John . . . help me . . . something's caught me . . ."

There was a blinding flash of lightning, and, by its lurid glare, the fear-paralysed watchers saw that there was another figure in the room . . . someone had come from somewhere . . . and had seized Elsie round the waist.

She straggled for an instant, and then collapsed into a limp heap which the intruder still gripped round the waist.

It was then that they all saw the face, and one and all recognised *Sir Charles Dorsay.*

He had come back from the land of the departed as Hampton had foretold. His face was demoniac in its snarling bestiality: and it was giggling to itself as it dragged Elsie away into the blackness.

No one could see more. But, with the exception of Richardson, who, having never seen Dorsay in the flesh, was not impressed by the vision as were all the others, everybody recognised him instantaneously.

Corbin and the maids had rushed from the place shrieking, and John Tarren would have flown, too; but for his love for Elsie. In one supreme moment of inspired bravery, he leapt forward with blazing eyes, and seized the girl himself, dragging her from those vile skeleton hands, and standing over her.

"Damn you—damn your accursed soul!" he thundered at the apparition. "Get back to the dead—she is mine, I tell you, *mine . . . mine . . .*"

His voice broke and the floor came up and hit him.

Almost at the same moment Richardson felt his up to now forgotten automatic pistol.

As a final, desperate, bid for life and sanity, he drew it from his pocket, and fired shot after shot at the living-dead figure of Sir Charles Dorsay.

CHAPTER XIII

THE RANGE FROM WHICH Richardson fired his shot was a very short one—not much more than about ten or eleven feet—so his bullets could hardly have gone astray unless, indeed, he had fired at something invulnerable by earthly weapons.

So he heard the bullets strike something solid with a soft series of thuds, and the figure fell to the ground with a sharp yell of pain.

This restored Richardson's lost nerve. He knew, in an instant, that he was dealing with no shadow from the great unknown: no horrible materialisation of a mediaeval superstition, but with an ordinary human being.

He knew, in one moment of thankfulness, that his instincts had not failed him, and the knowledge made him a man again. He pulled out his torch, put it on, and began to search for some means of getting the lights on.

He was not long in finding what he sought. Behind the prostrate and groaning figure he had shot down, was a wide opening in the oak paneling of the lounge. A beam from the torch inside the door revealed a switchboard and electric fuses; one of the fuses had been pulled right out of its socket, thus plunging the whole house into darkness. Richardson pushed it back, and the place was flooded once more with light.

He went up to the prostrate man who was groaning with pain, and, producing a couple of pairs of handcuffs, fettered both his arms and his ankles.

Then, without doing anything to relieve the prisoner's evident pain, Richardson picked up the still unconscious Elsie and laid her on the settee, pouring water over her face from the soda-syphon on the side-table.

Then he picked up Tarren, and forced some whisky between his lips after he had put him down on the tiger skin hearthrug and switched on the electric fire.

John came to first and stared wildly around him.

"It's all right, Tarren," said Richardson. "I have laid the family ghost forever."

John mutely pointed to the handcuffed man.

"That's no vampire," laughed Richardson, "that is a man of flesh and blood—a crook who has paid the price of being caught in his own trap."

John staggered to his feet. "Thank God," he gasped, and went over to where Elsie was just opening her eyes.

"It's all right darling," he whispered, "you are safe—quite safe with me."

Elsie clung to him like a frightened child.

"Well, now let's get this fellow into a safe place," laughed Richardson, and, going up to the man, who was tall and elderly, and in full evening-dress, he said, sharply:—

"Who are you, and what have you done with the body of Sir Charles Dorsay?"

"Help me," moaned the man weakly. "You got me and I'm dying . . ."

"Dying, eh," snapped Richardson. "No doubt—do you know you have been directly or indirectly responsible for the death of four people to my knowledge?" Then, with a faint touch of pity, he held a glass of whisky and water to the man's purple lips.

He drank thirstily and groaned again.

"Now then," said the detective—"Who are you?—you may as well tell the whole truth since you are caught and may not live to be tried."

"I am—*Sir Charles Dorsay,*" replied the man.

"What!" roared Richardson. "Why I have been investigating the death of Sir Charles Dorsay and have seen his dead body with my own eyes."

"I am Sir Charles Dorsay," again insisted the dying man weakly.

John Tarren gathered his wits together and went up to the prostrate man. A glance at the face was enough. It *was* Sir Charles.

"Yes, Inspector," he said. "This is Sir Charles Dorsay all right: unless he has an exact double."

"But you identified the dead man this morning as being Dorsay," cried Richardson, "they can't both be the fellow. He must be an impostor."

"This is Sir Charles, right enough," said Tarren. And Elsie identified him, too—after a brief shuddering glance from the shelter of her lover's arms.

Richardson bent over the dying man. "If you are Sir Charles Dorsay," said he, "tell me who was that man who was found shot dead in your library this morning and whose body disappeared to-night?"

Almost at the same instant there was a sharp cry from John who, pointing to the open panel, said:

"Look—look—there is the body!" Richardson rushed into the opening and dragged out a bundle in a blood-stained sheet.

It was a body in evening-dress of exactly the same make and condition as that which Dorsay was wearing, and the dead man was of precisely the same build. Their faces might have once been alike or not. It was impossible to say as the corpse, as we all know, had its face blown away to pulp.

This had made it impossible to swear to its identity. But it looked so like Dorsay that anyone, finding such a body in the place they had left the living baronet, would, without hesitation, have identified it as Sir Charles Dorsay with his face blown away.

Richardson made a brief examination of this macabre find, and said shortly:—

"This is the body that disappeared from the library, all right, but who is it, I wonder, and how the hell did it get in there? You put it there I suppose?" he finished, addressing Sir Charles.

Dorsay answered that he had.

"Who was this man—and who killed him?"

"I killed him," said Sir Charles. "I knew you would take him for me."

"Why did you want to be thought dead?"

"I wanted to disappear . . . I was ruined . . . and he . . . he . . ." pointing to John Tarren, "stole Elsie's love from me . . . and I wanted to send him to the gallows for my murder . . ."

Bit by bit the tale came out and Richardson took it down. Dorsay was dying fast, and his words came in gasps and scraps. Sometimes he was inaudible, and sometimes he only rambled away into nonsense.

But, at last, the whole confession was got from him, and a complicated and strange tale it was too. It was also quite a masterpiece of cunning.

Here it is rendered into readable shape.

The lawyer Hampton had spoken the truth when he had said that Sir Charles Dorsay was ruined. So he was: utterly ruined. In fact he had not only lost his whole fortune on a stock exchange gamble, but, in a vain attempt to recover some of it, embezzled the whole of Elsie's £5,000 as well.

He had, as we already know, developed an insane passion for his ward, and when, on top of his money troubles, she refused to marry him, it fairly unbalanced his never too stable mind—especially when he found that she loved John Tarren—his secretary, and "his hireling," as he mentally thought of the young fellow.

Naturally enough, he loathed his rival, and the desire to revenge himself very soon overmastered every other interest Dorsay had in life. He brooded over it night and day, until, at last, he determined to kill the man, and avoid both the disgrace of having to face his own financial crash and the charge of murder by killing himself afterwards. He hoped to re-act on Elsie's feelings too by robbing her of her lover and making her feel responsible for her guardian's suicide. She would be quite penniless, too, as even the old manor was mortgaged up to the hilt.

He planned the whole thing out in his mind, and, finally, decided to do the deed by poison. He obtained a supply of one of the worst poisons known to science—*Cyanide of Potassium*—by representing to the chemist that he wanted it for the destruction of butterflies for his collection. As this poison is very largely employed by naturalists for this purpose he did not find any great difficulty in obtaining it.

At another chemist's shop he purchased a hypodermic syringe of large size with a fine needle. He intended to dissolve the poison in water and to fill the syringe with the deadly liquid. Then he could creep behind John as he sat writing at a table, drive the needle home into the back of his neck, press the piston in and the terrible poison would do its work in a few seconds. A poison injected into the blood in this way is twice as deadly as a poison taken in the ordinary way.

When Tarren was dead he could take a dose himself and all would be over.

When in this way everything was ready for the crime something happened which made Dorsay alter his whole scheme, and make it far more terrible and subtle and at the same time avoid hurting himself.

What happened was this. When Dorsay was taking a walk in the village and turning the diabolical scheme over in his mind, he was accosted by a beggar who asked for alms. Sir Charles noticed that the beggar was exactly his own build, and, approximately, the same age; and overheard two passing women on the road remark about the similarity between the two men and comment on the sad difference between their circumstances.

In an instant Sir Charles Dorsay had an inspiration. It was a kind of flash of criminal genius.

If this beggar had his face blown away in some way his dead body might easily be mistaken for that of Sir Charles himself.

So Sir Charles decided to get the man to "Dorsay Hall" somehow in the night, kill him with the cyanide he had prepared for Tarren, and smash his face in by firing a shot-gun right into it.

He would then hide himself in a secret room in the old manor known only to himself—it was none other than the

walled up bedroom of his ancestor, Sir Phillip Dorsay, referred to in the *Dorsay Manuscript*—and which communi-
cated with the library, the lounge, and the garage, by means
of sliding panels.

As soon as he could hear from his hiding-place how the
land lay he would slip out of his retreat and be off to the
Continent.

He determined to dress the beggar in a suit of his clothes
and sit him at the desk in the room when he was dead. Any
person who had left Sir Charles himself living sitting there
one night, and finding a similar figure dressed in exactly the
same way in the same position the next morning, would be
sure to declare that the body was that of Sir Charles.

Anyhow the thing would work quite long enough to en-
able him to get away, and he could always kill himself if
captured and be no worse off than he would be if he kept to
his original plan.

But the chance of his being captured was small since people do not as a rule examine the bodies of murdered or self-
destroyed relatives to see if they are the bodies of someone
else disguised to deceive—unless they have some very good
reason for suspecting such deceit.

And, in this case, there was no reason at all for such a deceit as far as everyone knew. Instead there was everything
that would point to a desire for suicide.

But Sir Charles wanted it to point to *murder* if possible,
and so get John hanged.

So he made all the necessary arrangements. He first of all
entered his secret room and put there a bag with sufficient
clothes for his immediate needs, a supply of food and a lamp.
The room could be lighted at night without the light being
seen.

Next he provided himself with a duplicate key to the library.

Then he set about involving Tarren in the matter. Corbin
had been spying on the couple for some time past, and Dorsay determined to catch the lovers together, and then taunt
John into striking him or saying something that might go

against him—such as threaten to kill him, etc. He determined to openly insult the lovers and state his intention of altering his will in Elsie's disfavour in the presence of Corbin, and thus provide a witness against him.

Dorsay knew that, if he died on the very night following a violent quarrel, and that his death had seemed to prevent him altering his will, which, otherwise, would seem to bring John a fortune through Elsie, it would look very black against the man who stood to gain by his death—especially in view of the quarrel.

So, as we know, Sir Charles did catch the lovers together, and he did goad John into both threatening him and striking him.

So far so good.

As soon as he was alone in the library, Dorsay locked himself in, and wrote out part of an altered will in Elsie's disfavour. He had instructed the beggar to visit him, and given him the key to a back entrance to the grounds of the manor, promising him five hundred pounds for some service or other.

The beggar turned up to the moment. Dorsay gave the man a meal of cheese, biscuits, and whisky. The whisky contained a generous dose of cyanide of potassium.

Two seconds later the man was stone dead.

Dorsay stripped off the man's clothes and dressed him in his own evening clothes, draping himself in another suit he had in his safe for that purpose.

He sat the body at the table, and then carefully hid every trace of a second party having entered the room. The man's own clothes he packed in a bag and took away into his secret room when he left.

But first he took down a shot-gun, and blew in the face of the already dead man.

He knew that the report of the gun might rouse the household, and so he left it to the very last—knowing that he could throw down the gun and vanish through the already open panel into the secret passage that led to his walled-up room, closing the panel immediately after him. Not a soul in the world knew that there was such a thing save Dorsay himself.

But, oddly enough, the commotion he expected to follow the shot did not come about.

He laughed to himself with glee. He was extra lucky. Apparently nobody had heard anything.

He put the gun down where it might be expected to fall from the hands of a suicide, or be flung down by a murderer. He knew that expert examination of the room would reveal that it was more like a murder than a suicide, and things pointed to John since he or Elsie were the only people to gain by the death of Sir Charles Dorsay.

Putting together his things Dorsay made a discovery which again altered his plans. And it was this alteration which ultimately destroyed him.

For had he merely slipped away into his hiding-place, and made his get-away the night following the murder, just before the inquest, the thing might never have come to light. The beggar might have been buried as Sir Charles Dorsay.

But, as it was, Dorsay found in one of his desk drawers a little key.

It was the key to Elsie's bedroom. A duplicate Sir Charles himself had had made some time before. We need not ask for what purpose.

Now it gave him an idea. He would not make his get-away as soon as he had intended to. He would wait in his secret room, and, as the passage led right round the old Manor House, he could listen and see how things were progressing. In the middle of the night he would creep out of his hiding-place, and kill Elsie with his hypodermic syringe and solution of cyanide of potassium.

He determined that—"if he could not have her nobody should," in fact.

Of course, the man was not quite sane, and even his cunning was leaving him. But he could still think after a fashion. He had reason enough to know that he would run a risk of being caught. And that would mean that *he* might be hanged.

Then he remembered the old legend of the Dorsay *vampires*.

Let them see him alive—when they thought him dead—let them. They would only think that he had become a vampire. It might frighten them from further enquiry.

But the thing would have to be done properly.

So he set to work to do it in the best way he could. He knew that old Hampton not only knew of the "family curse" but believed in it as an article of faith. He remembered that when his own father died Hampton had insisted upon the vampire rites being performed on the body. Sir Charles had given in, and the thing had been done without the knowledge of anyone by Hampton himself and Sir Charles who, being intoxicated at the time, looked upon it as a kind of joke.

Hampton, no doubt, would insist again, and bring up the whole story.

But, in case of accidents, Sir Charles laid the *Dorsay Manuscript* on the table—and even went so far as to smear the cover with the beggar's blood, and arrange the dead hand as if it were holding the book at the time of its death.

He knew that the police would never consent to vampire rites being observed, and he determined to show them that "there were such things as vampires."

When he had killed Elsie he would make two little cuts in her throat with a pocket razor.

All this flashed through Dorsay's mind in an instant, and it was not five minutes from the time the gun was fired to the time he closed the sliding panel after him and vanished into his secret room.

Luckily for Tarren, Richardson inclined to the theory of suicide rather than of murder, and Hampton's statement of Dorsay's ruin confirmed him in this conclusion.

Sir Charles, from behind the paneling of the lounge, had heard his hated secretary slip out of the noose he had prepared for him, and gnashed his teeth with fury. He had forgotten that Hampton knew about his financial collapse.

But, if one revenge had failed him, another would still be his. He would kill Elsie and that would react upon Tarren all right.

And Dorsay laughed silently to himself.

He heard how the vampire tale made itself known: he heard how it was received. He heard everyone go to bed, and listened to Richardson putting the constables on guard.

This was just what he wanted. He would scare everyone. The matter of the cat was a pure coincidence—one of those coincidences which keep superstitions alive—and Dorsay was delighted when he heard about it.

When all was quiet he crept along the passage until he stood behind the panel which led into the library, and gently slid it back.

There was a village policeman he knew well asleep under the french window.

He must be killed first.

Dorsay had crept up to the man and bent over him when the policeman woke up. Seeing an apparently dead man alive in front of him, and this coming on top of the legend—which had impressed him not a little—the policeman's tired brain well-nigh turned, and he fled out through the french windows. But he had woken a little too late, and the needle had pricked him.

A very tiny drop of the poison got into a scratch made by the needle, and the violent exercise of running did the rest. Bates's heart stopped, but as luck would have it not until he had told of what he had seen in the library.

Having got rid of one of the constables, Dorsay unlocked the door from inside with his duplicate key. He did so very quietly, and as the second policeman was asleep it did not wake him.

Dorsay slid a head and hand out of the half-opened door, and gave Rowlands a full dose of the cyanide which killed him outright on the spot.

Then he went back into the library, and, in an instant, had slid the beggar's body off the table into the cavity behind the sliding panel, which he closed.

Then, after listening and finding all quiet, he crept across the lounge, upstairs, and got into Elsie's bedroom. It was now that he made another blunder. He did not know that Vesta was sharing Elsie's bed: he had missed the arrangement somehow, He fumbled about and found the wrong woman's throat with his poison-needle.

Hence it came about that Vesta was killed and Elsie escaped. Dorsay made two little gashes in the dead throat with his razor, and it was then Elsie woke up and screamed.

The same flash of lightning as revealed his presence to Elsie also showed him the blunder he had done.

There was only one thing to be done and he did it as he heard Tarren outside the door—which he had locked inside after he had got into the room—Dorsay escaped through the window which opened on to a balcony, and managed to slide down a drainpipe to the ground.

Once there he dashed round the house to the garage of which he had the key, and from within there once again entered "Dorsay Hall," and was back again into his secret room before he could be seen.

But it was a severe physical effort for an old man and only the dire necessity which galvanised him to action enabled him to do it.

Although it would at any other time have exhausted him, yet now in view of his failure in his object Dorsay did not feel tired. Mind conquered body.

But it was by now the mind of a man who had really passed across that indefinite borderland between sanity and insanity. Sir Charles was really mad now, and so it was not very long before he gave himself away.

Elsie was still alive. Tarren still uncharged with murder. John must not have Elsie at any cost. She must be killed!

But how? He had failed, and she would not be left alone again.

He must kidnap her and get her into his secret room and there kill her.

But how?

He thought at first he would put out all the lights and throw the beggar's body out of the panel that led to the lounge.

This would scare everybody out of the house—Elsie too. But in the confusion he might be able to abduct her.

He dragged the body to the right position—just inside the panel that led into the lounge and listened.

He could put the lights out easily enough. The lounge panel led into a cupboard where there was the main switch and the fuse-box. He crept into the cupboard and gently pushed the door—it was unlocked.

Fortune favoured him. He could get into the lounge from his hiding-place in that passage.

Then he heard the return and death of Bates, and also heard Richardson suggest leaving the house.

They were going. Elsie was going too. He had not a second to lose.

He forgot about the body which he had dragged into the cupboard in readiness, reached up his hand, pulled out the main fuse of the house, heard the screams and confusion, and burst out into the lounge.

He very nearly succeeded in capturing the girl as we know. Had it not been for Tarren's bravery in tearing her from the arms of what he, at that moment, thought to be a being from another world, he might have escaped into his cupboard, and thence into his passage, and from thence into his secret room, before anyone recovered from their paralysis of fear and superstition seemingly proved.

The interior of the cupboard gave not the least indication of a false back, and the body of the beggar lying in there would have only spread more superstitious terror than existed already.

But as it was the delay was just enough for Richardson to galvanise his brain back to reason in the emergency and use his revolver.

And so Sir Charles Dorsay died in reality, who had faked death for the greater part of a night.

Detective-Inspector Richardson laid the head of the *really dead* Sir Charles Dorsay on the ground and rose to his feet, after he had managed, with great difficulty, to piece together the above narrative which gave the clue to all those strange and terrible happenings which had brought so much death and so much fear within that old Manor House during this unholy night, from the last words of the cause of it all.

"Dorsay has gone to his account," he said briefly, "the last of the line of vampire-baronets is dead: he will trouble this earth no more."

He dragged the form of Bates to the side of that of the late Sir Charles, laid the two bodies side by side: dust to dust: ashes to ashes, and covered them over with his own great-coat.

"And now," said he to John Tarren, who was standing by with his arm round Elsie, who, although still white and shaken from her recent nerve-wrackings, was rapidly recovering her old spirit, "now all the superstition has been done away with once and for all, and the family ghost effectively laid, let's go and see where that rat has been hiding."

John assented, although without any great enthusiasm, and Elsie volunteered to come with them.

The trio entered the little cupboard, and, making their way to the back, began to investigate. It was not long before they found the sliding panel and got it open.

They entered the great cavity in the wall it revealed, Richardson putting on his electric torch and guiding the way. There was a passage roughly seven feet in height and just wide enough for them to proceed along in single file. It led in both directions.

Drawing a bow at a venture, they followed the right hand path and found that it led them right round the house. The walls of the passage were of very ancient stone on the outer and age-blackened oak on the inner. It had evidently been constructed by the builders of "Dorsay Hall" to the order of old Sir Phillip Dorsay, though exactly for what purpose it was difficult to imagine. No doubt he wanted to have a secret means of escape from the Manor if, for some reason or other, he should have found it necessary to fly.

Richardson sounded both the inner and the outer walls very thoroughly and found them for the most part quite solid. He was looking for the other panels which gave admission from the passage to other rooms in the house.

It was not long before he found the one which led into the library: this one, however, was not an ordinary sliding panel, but a heavy oaken door bolted with massive oaken bolts from the inside.

Drawing these from their sockets Richardson exerted his whole strength and pushed the door open, entering the library, and finding that the inside of this door was masked by a great bookcase full of heavy volumes.

"Ha," he smiled, "an old trick."

They entered the passage again, leaving the door open, and the library lights full on to guide them back, and continued their exploration.

A few yards further on was a narrow winding stone stair. "That leads to the walled-up bedroom," said the detective to his companions, "come along."

So they climbed up this tortuous stair, and, at the top, were checked by a wall of stone. But it was not long before Richardson looked above his head and said.

"You see—there is a trap-door this time."

He pushed the oaken ceiling above them and it yielded. It was a heavy oak trap-door in the floor of the walled-up bedroom of Sir Phillip Dorsay.

He opened it to its fullest extent, and drew himself up without much difficulty. John followed, and the two men between them helped Elsie after them.

Richardson flashed the torch round them.

Sure enough they were in the ancient room referred to in the old manuscript. They had, as Richardson guessed, entered it through the floor.

It was a large, gloomy, oak-beamed chamber of great age: furnished with a massive four-poster bed upon which still crumbled the remains of its original bedding which had been left there when it was walled up three hundred odd years before.

There was where the door once had led out to the landing. It had been blocked up with stone masonry and barricaded as if against an army. Opposite there was where there had once been a window. This, too, had been barricaded with stonework, so that the room had virtually disappeared for generations. Sir Charles had been the only man who knew of its existence—Sir Charles and Hampton. And, as Richardson found later on, Dorsay had located it from a plan in the old manuscript.

The old room, which, until Sir Charles had used it as a hiding place, had not been entered since the days of Henry VIII, was exactly as it had been abandoned. The massive antique furniture was crumbling with age and decay, and even the old floor was rotten in parts. One of the beams in the ceiling had fallen diagonally across the bed.

In one corner were the signs of its recent habitation by Sir Charles Dorsay. There was a leather Gladstone bag packed ready for his exit: a considerable supply of food, two boxes of cigars, a couple of dozen boxes of matches, a can of oil, and a high-pressure paraffin lamp, which was on the point of going out for want of oil.

Richardson filled it from the can and re-lighted it. In the brilliant illumination which it gave he made a careful examination of what Dorsay had collected there for his flight and his diabolical scheme of playing vampire.

There in a corner was a large bundle of dirty old clothes. Evidently these were the beggar's original garments.

Richardson possessed himself of these.

"They will be wanted at the inquest," said he. "Of course, this tramp must be identified, and his relatives, if any, traced."

He opened the leather traveling-bag, and went through its contents. There was nothing of any great interest. A couple of suits, an overcoat, some underclothing, and a passport for the Continent.

The passport, however, had been issued under a false name—Wilfred Reynaldson, solicitor, as had a first-class ticket for Calais.

In a leather wallet was about fifty pounds in notes, and about fifteen shillings' worth of silver.

"Apparently this and the ticket was all he was worth," said Richardson—"wonder how he intended living."

"He's evidently got rid of every penny of my money," said Elsie, "whatever shall we do, John dearest?"

"Work for a living, I suppose," he answered. "Don't mind much what we do so long as we are spared to each other."

"I suppose neither of you have a penny," said the detective.

Both admitted that they had not.

"Well, since Miss Mervyn is the sole legatee under Dorsay's will, she had better have this money—what there is of it," he replied, handing over the wallet and its contents.

Then again he said—half to himself.

"It's all very well Dorsay wanting to escape and start a new life at sixty on about fifty pounds odd. But that would not last a man of his habits long. What *did* he intend living on I wonder?"

As he spoke his foot kicked against a metal box standing in the deep shadow under the old carved chair on the crumbling seat of which he had stood Sir Charles' bag.

With a smothered exclamation he dragged it to the light. It was of great age and had recently been strapped across with a hold-all handle making it just possible to carry. And there was a luggage label pasted upon it indicating that it was to go to Calais.

What did it contain?

"He was evidently going to take this with him as well as his bag," said Richardson. "Let's get it open and see what is inside it."

But it was locked with a heavy padlock, and there was no key.

"He must have had the key," muttered John, "or he could not have opened it himself."

But, search as they would, no key could be found in the luggage Sir Charles had prepared for his flight.

"I know," said Elsie, "it's a ghoulish thought, I know, but don't you think that, as this box may contain something valuable, Sir Charles may have had the key on him."

"Good idea," said Richardson, "let's get the box down to the lounge."

They carted it down to the passage-way, closing the old trap-door behind them, Richardson carefully putting out the lamp in case of fire. The old room was left for the inspection of the Coroner.

Guided by the library lights they made their way back to the inhabited portion of the old house, and, as Elsie had suggested, there, in the waistcoat pocket of the dead Sir Charles, was the missing key.

But the lock was old and rusty and it was no light task to get it open. Still, by dint of much hard work, the ancient lid was at last raised.

And then what a sight met their eyes. The box was cram full of old gold and jewellery. There must have been about £40,000 worth or more.

All of it was marked with the Dorsay crest.

There can be little doubt but that this treasure-trove had been discovered by Sir Charles in the walled-up room and during his preparation of the place for his reception.

"It seems that you two young people are in luck's way," said Richardson, "you have lost your £5,000 Miss Mervyn, but there is quite that here in kind I should say."

There was only one thing more to be done—the outlet from the passage into the grounds had to be found, and, after a long and patient sounding, Richardson found it—a good twenty feet along the passage leading from the lounge entrance in the direction opposite to that which they had first taken.

It was a massive stone door bolted with oaken bolts from within, and leading outside the back of "Dorsay Hall."

"How easily he could have slipped away," meditated Richardson, "if only he had kept to his first intention of making his escape directly after dark to-night, instead of waiting to try to murder you, Miss Mervyn."

"And since he would have been thought dead and buried, how little disguise would have sufficed for him to get to France, have his treasure melted down, realise the money, and live the rest of his life free from his creditors," he continued, when they all were back again in the lounge.

"Still," said John "it's a good thing that criminals like that nearly always over-reach themselves."

"It is," replied the detective, "they get over-confident and give themselves away at last. But I think Dorsay actually lost his reason—his mind gave way and something snapped in his brain, no doubt. He was evidently fired with the notion that he was omnipotent—he thought, at last, in his ravings, that he really *was* the vampire he was enacting. And so he perished."

"Still," said John, "he managed to explain everything before he died, and he seemed sane enough then . . ."

"Ah yes," said Richardson, "no doubt the shock of those bullets pulled his scattered wits together. And you must remember that his insanity took the fairly common form of pride in his crime. He did not want to die without anyone knowing how clever he had been. I think that this alone gave him strength to last long enough to make his confession."

"God, what a night it has been," said John Tarren, dropping exhausted on a chair, and burying his face in his hands. "It's a wonder that we were not all driven mad."

"Another half-hour—nay fifteen minutes of that horror when it seemed that hell had really come to earth," said the detective, "and we certainly would have been maniacs—but a merciful Providence gave out that it was not to be."

"I shall never forget this terrible night—never," said Elsie, "its terror will haunt my dreams as long as I live."

"Even on your honeymoon?" asked Richardson.

Elsie laughed, and blushed, "Well, perhaps not then . . ."

She laid her hand on John's head. "Dear old boy—if it hadn't been for you . . ."

John gathered her up in his arms and kissed her passionately: unmindful of the presence of the detective—who had lighted his pipe and was puffing contentedly.

"Let's forget all about it, dearest, hear the dry old inquest through, and then go right away from this old place and be happy together forever."

"Yes, let's," came in smothered tones from the shoulder of Tarren's coat.

Richardson yawned, and walked across to the old window. It was nearly broad daylight although no one yet realised it.

The Inspector drew aside the heavy curtains, jerked the window open, and pointed with his pipe to the crimson streaks of the rising sun.

"Look," he said, "here comes the dawn." He mopped his brow with his handkerchief, and drew in a deep breath of the early morning air, saying, as he did so:

"Lord, I've never been more thankful to see the daylight!"

RAMBLE HOUSE's

HARRY STEPHEN KEELER WEBWORK MYSTERIES

(RH) indicates the title is available ONLY in the RAMBLE HOUSE edition

The Ace of Spades Murder
The Affair of the Bottled Deuce (RH)
The Amazing Web
The Barking Clock
Behind That Mask
The Book with the Orange Leaves
The Bottle with the Green Wax Seal
The Box from Japan
The Case of the Canny Killer
The Case of the Crazy Corpse (RH)
The Case of the Flying Hands (RH)
The Case of the Ivory Arrow
The Case of the Jeweled Ragpicker
The Case of the Lavender Gripsack
The Case of the Mysterious Moll
The Case of the 16 Beans
The Case of the Transparent Nude (RH)
The Case of the Transposed Legs
The Case of the Two-Headed Idiot (RH)
The Case of the Two Strange Ladies
The Circus Stealers (RH)
Cleopatra's Tears
A Copy of Beowulf (RH)
The Crimson Cube (RH)
The Face of the Man From Saturn
Find the Clock
The Five Silver Buddhas
The 4th King
The Gallows Waits, My Lord! (RH)
The Green Jade Hand
Finger! Finger!
Hangman's Nights (RH)
I, Chameleon (RH)
I Killed Lincoln at 10:13! (RH)
The Iron Ring
The Man Who Changed His Skin (RH)
The Man with the Crimson Box
The Man with the Magic Eardrums
The Man with the Wooden Spectacles
The Marceau Case
The Matilda Hunter Murder
The Monocled Monster

The Murder of London Lew
The Murdered Mathematician
The Mysterious Card (RH)
The Mysterious Ivory Ball of Wong Shing Li
  (RH)
The Mystery of the Fiddling Cracksman
The Peacock Fan
The Photo of Lady X (RH)
The Portrait of Jirjohn Cobb
Report on Vanessa Hewstone (RH)
Riddle of the Travelling Skull
Riddle of the Wooden Parrakeet (RH)
The Scarlet Mummy (RH)
The Search for X-Y-Z
The Sharkskin Book
Sing Sing Nights
The Six From Nowhere (RH)
The Skull of the Waltzing Clown
The Spectacles of Mr. Cagliostro
Stand By—London Calling!
The Steeltown Strangler
The Stolen Gravestone (RH)
Strange Journey (RH)
The Strange Will
The Straw Hat Murders (RH)
The Street of 1000 Eyes (RH)
Thieves' Nights
Three Novellos (RH)
The Tiger Snake
The Trap (RH)
Vagabond Nights (Defrauded Yeggman)
Vagabond Nights 2 (10 Hours)
The Vanishing Gold Truck
The Voice of the Seven Sparrows
The Washington Square Enigma
When Thief Meets Thief
The White Circle (RH)
The Wonderful Scheme of Mr. Christopher
  Thorne
X. Jones—of Scotland Yard
Y. Cheung, Business Detective

Keeler Related Works

A To Izzard: A Harry Stephen Keeler Companion by Fender Tucker — Articles and stories
  about Harry, by Harry, and in his style. Included is a compleat bibliography.
Wild About Harry: Reviews of Keeler Novels — Edited by Richard Polt & Fender Tucker —
  22 reviews of works by Harry Stephen Keeler from *Keeler News*. A perfect introduction to the
  author.
The Keeler Keyhole Collection: Annotated newsletter rants from Harry Stephen Keeler,
  edited by Francis M. Nevins. Over 400 pages of incredibly personal Keeleriana.
Fakealoo — Pastiches of the style of Harry Stephen Keeler by selected demented members
  of the HSK Society. Updated every year with the new winner.
Strands of the Web: Short Stories of Harry Stephen Keeler — 29 stories, just about all that
  Keeler wrote, are edited and introduced by Fred Cleaver.

RAMBLE HOUSE's Loon Sanctuary

A Clear Path to Cross — Sharon Knowles short mystery stories by Ed Lynskey.

A Jimmy Starr Omnibus — Three 40s novels by Jimmy Starr.

A Roland Daniel Double: The Signal and The Return of Wu Fang — Classic thrillers from the 30s.

A Shot Rang Out — Three decades of reviews and articles by today's Anthony Boucher, Jon Breen. An essential book for any mystery lover's library.

A Smell of Smoke — A 1951 English countryside thriller by Miles Burton.

A Snark Selection — Lewis Carroll's *The Hunting of the Snark* with two Snarkian chapters by Harry Stephen Keeler — Illustrated by Gavin L. O'Keefe.

A Young Man's Heart — A forgotten early classic by Cornell Woolrich.

Alexander Laing Novels — *The Motives of Nicholas Holtz* and *Dr. Scarlett*, stories of medical mayhem and intrigue from the 30s.

An Angel in the Street — Modern hardboiled noir by Peter Genovese.

Automaton — Brilliant treatise on robotics: 1928-style! By H. Stafford Hatfield.

Beast or Man? — A 1930 novel of racism and horror by Sean M'Guire. Introduced by John Pelan.

Black Hogan Strikes Again — Australia's Peter Renwick pens a tale of the 30s outback.

Black River Falls — Suspense from the master, Ed Gorman.

Blondy's Boy Friend — A snappy 1930 story by Philip Wylie, writing as Leatrice Homesley.

Blood in a Snap — The *Finnegan's Wake* of the 21st century, by Jim Weiler.

Blood Moon — The first of the Robert Payne series by Ed Gorman.

Chelsea Quinn Yarbro Novels featuring Charlie Moon — *Ogilvie, Tallant and Moon, Music When the Sweet Voice Dies, Poisonous Fruit* and *Dead Mice*. An Ojibwa detective in SF.

Cornucopia of Crime — Francis M. Nevins assembled this huge collection of his writings about crime literature and the people who write it. Essential for any serious mystery library.

Crimson Clown Novels — By Johnston McCulley, author of the Zorro novels, *The Crimson Clown* and *The Crimson Clown Again*.

Dago Red — 22 tales of dark suspense by Bill Pronzini.

David Hume Novels — *Corpses Never Argue, Cemetery First Stop, Make Way for the Mourners, Eternity Here I Come*. 1930s British hardboiled fiction with an attitude.

Dead Man Talks Too Much — Hollywood boozer by Weed Dickenson.

Death Leaves No Card — One of the most unusual murdered-in-the-tub mysteries you'll ever read. By Miles Burton.

Death March of the Dancing Dolls and Other Stories — Volume Three in the Day Keene in the Detective Pulps series. Introduced by Bill Crider.

Deep Space and other Stories — A collection of SF gems by Richard A. Lupoff.

Detective Duff Unravels It — Episodic mysteries by Harvey O'Higgins.

Dime Novels: Ramble House's 10-Cent Books — *Knife in the Dark* by Robert Leslie Bellem, *Hot Lead* and *Song of Death* by Ed Earl Repp, *A Hashish House in New York* by H.H. Kane, and five more.

Don Diablo: Book of a Lost Film — Two-volume treatment of a western by Paul Landres, with diagrams. Intro by Francis M. Nevins.

Dope and Swastikas — Two strange novels from 1922 by Edmund Snell

Dope Tales #1 — Two dope-riddled classics; *Dope Runners* by Gerald Grantham and *Death Takes the Joystick* by Phillip Condé.

Dope Tales #2 — Two more narco-classics; *The Invisible Hand* by Rex Dark and *The Smokers of Hashish* by Norman Berrow.

Dope Tales #3 — Two enchanting novels of opium by the master, Sax Rohmer. *Dope* and *The Yellow Claw*.

Double Hot — Two 60s softcore sex novels by Morris Hershman.

Dr. Odin — Douglas Newton's 1933 racial potboiler comes back to life.

Evidence in Blue — 1938 mystery by E. Charles Vivian.

Fatal Accident — Murder by automobile, a 1936 mystery by Cecil M. Wills.

Finger-prints Never Lie — A 1939 classic detective novel by John G. Brandon.

Freaks and Fantasies — Eerie tales by Tod Robbins, collaborator of Tod Browning on the film FREAKS.

Gadsby — A lipogram (a novel without the letter E). Ernest Vincent Wright's last work, published in 1939 right before his death.

Gelett Burgess Novels — *The Master of Mysteries, The White Cat, Two O'Clock Courage, Ladies in Boxes, Find the Woman, The Heart Line, The Picaroons* and *Lady Mechante*. All are introduced by Richard A. Lupoff who is singlehandedly bringing Burgess back to life.

Geronimo — S. M. Barrett's 1905 autobiography of a noble American.

Hake Talbot Novels — *Rim of the Pit, The Hangman's Handyman*. Classic locked room mysteries, with mapback covers by Gavin O'Keefe.

Hollywood Dreams — A novel of Tinsel Town and the Depression by Richard O'Brien.

I Stole $16,000,000 — A true story by cracksman Herbert E. Wilson.

Inclination to Murder — 1966 thriller by New Zealand's Harriet Hunter.

Invaders from the Dark — Classic werewolf tale from Greye La Spina.

J. Poindexter, Colored — Classic satirical black novel by Irvin S. Cobb.

Jack Mann Novels — Strange murder in the English countryside. *Gees' First Case, Nightmare Farm, Grey Shapes, The Ninth Life, The Glass Too Many*.

Jake Hardy — A lusty western tale from Wesley Tallant.

Jim Harmon Double Novels — *Vixen Hollow/Celluloid Scandal, The Man Who Made Maniacs/Silent Siren, Ape Rape/Wanton Witch, Sex Burns Like Fire/Twist Session, Sudden Lust/Passion Strip, Sin Unlimited/Harlot Master, Twilight Girls/Sex Institution*. Written in the early 60s and never reprinted until now.

Joel Townsley Rogers Novels and Short Stories — By the author of *The Red Right Hand: Once In a Red Moon, Lady With the Dice, The Stopped Clock, Never Leave My Bed*. Also two short story collections: *Night of Horror* and *Killing Time*.

Joseph Shallit Novels — *The Case of the Billion Dollar Body, Lady Don't Die on My Doorstep, Kiss the Killer, Yell Bloody Murder, Take Your Last Look*. One of America's best 50's authors and a favorite of author Bill Pronzini.

Keller Memento — 45 short stories of the amazing and weird by Dr. David Keller.

Killer's Caress — Cary Moran's 1936 hardboiled thriller.

League of the Grateful Dead and Other Stories — Volume One in the Day Keene in the Detective Pulps series. In the introduction John Pelan outlines his plans for re-publishing all of Day Keene's short stories from the pulps.

Man Out of Hell and Other Stories — Volume II of the John H. Knox weird pulps collection.

Marblehead: A Novel of H.P. Lovecraft — A long-lost masterpiece from Richard A. Lupoff. This is the "director's cut", the long version that has never been published before.

Master of Souls — Mark Hansom's 1937 shocker is introduced by weirdologist John Pelan.

Max Afford Novels — *Owl of Darkness, Death's Mannikins, Blood on His Hands, The Dead Are Blind, The Sheep and the Wolves, Sinners in Paradise* and *Two Locked Room Mysteries and a Ripping Yarn* by one of Australia's finest mystery novelists.

More Secret Adventures of Sherlock Holmes — Gary Lovisi's second collection of tales about the unknown sides of the great detective.

Muddled Mind: Complete Works of Ed Wood, Jr. — David Hayes and Hayden Davis deconstruct the life and works of the mad, but canny, genius.

Murder among the Nudists — A mystery from 1934 by Peter Hunt, featuring a naked Detective-Inspector going undercover in a nudist colony.

Murder in Black and White — 1931 classic tennis whodunit by Evelyn Elder.

Murder in Shawnee — Two novels of the Alleghenies by John Douglas: *Shawnee Alley Fire* and *Haunts*.

Murder in Silk — A 1937 Yellow Peril novel of the silk trade by Ralph Trevor.

My Deadly Angel — 1955 Cold War drama by John Chelton.

My First Time: The One Experience You Never Forget — Michael Birchwood — 64 true first-person narratives of how they lost it.

Mysterious Martin, the Master of Murder — Two versions of a strange 1912 novel by Tod Robbins about a man who writes books that can kill.

Norman Berrow Novels — *The Bishop's Sword, Ghost House, Don't Go Out After Dark, Claws of the Cougar, The Smokers of Hashish, The Secret Dancer, Don't Jump Mr. Boland!, The Footprints of Satan, Fingers for Ransom, The Three Tiers of Fantasy, The Spaniard's Thumb, The Eleventh Plague, Words Have Wings, One Thrilling Night, The Lady's in Danger, It Howls at Night, The Terror in the Fog, Oil Under the Window, Murder in the Melody, The Singing Room.* This is the complete Norman Berrow library of classic locked-room mysteries, several of which are masterpieces.

Old Times' Sake — Short stories by James Reasoner from Mike Shayne Magazine.

Perfect .38 — Two early Timothy Dane novels by William Ard. More to come.

Prose Bowl — Futuristic satire of a world where hack writing has replaced football as our national obsession, by Bill Pronzini and Barry N. Malzberg.

Red Light — The history of legal prostitution in Shreveport Louisiana by Eric Brock. Includes wonderful photos of the houses and the ladies.

Researching American-Made Toy Soldiers — A 276-page collection of a lifetime of articles by toy soldier expert Richard O'Brien.

Reunion in Hell — Volume One of the John H. Knox series of weird stories from the pulps. Introduced by horror expert John Pelan.

Ripped from the Headlines! — The Jack the Ripper story as told in the newspaper articles in the *New York* and *London Times.*

Robert Randisi Novels — *No Exit to Brooklyn* and *The Dead of Brooklyn.* The first two Nick Delvecchio novels.

Rough Cut & New, Improved Murder — Ed Gorman's first two novels.

Ruled By Radio — 1925 futuristic novel by Robert L. Hadfield & Frank E. Farncombe.

Rupert Penny Novels — *Policeman's Holiday, Policeman's Evidence, Lucky Policeman, Policeman in Armour, Sealed Room Murder, Sweet Poison, The Talkative Policeman, She had to Have Gas* and *Cut and Run* (by Martin Tanner.) Rupert Penny is the pseudonym of Australian Charles Thornett, a master of the locked room, impossible crime plot.

Sand's Game — Spectacular hard-boiled noir from Ennis Willie, edited by Lynn Myers and Stephen Mertz, with contributions from Max Allan Collins, Bill Crider, Wayne Dundee, Bill Pronzini, Gary Lovisi and James Reasoner.

Satan's Den Exposed — True crime in Truth or Consequences New Mexico — Award-winning journalism by the *Desert Journal.*

Gelett Burgess Novels — *The Master of Mysteries, The White Cat, Two O'Clock Courage, Ladies in Boxes, Find the Woman, The Heart Line, The Picaroons* and *Lady Mechante.* All are edited and introduced by Richard A. Lupoff.

Sam McCain Novels — Ed Gorman's terrific series includes *The Day the Music Died, Wake Up Little Susie* and *Will You Still Love Me Tomorrow?*

Sex Slave — Potboiler of lust in the days of Cleopatra by Dion Leclerq, 1966.

Shadows' Edge — Two early novels by Wade Wright: *Shadows Don't Bleed* and *The Sharp Edge.*

Sideslip — 1968 SF masterpiece by Ted White and Dave Van Arnam.

Slammer Days — Two full-length prison memoirs: *Men into Beasts* (1952) by George Sylvester Viereck and *Home Away From Home* (1962) by Jack Woodford.

Sorcerer's Chessmen — John Pelan introduces this 1939 classic by Mark Hansom.

Star Griffin — Michael Kurland's 1987 masterpiece of SF drollery is back.

Stakeout on Millennium Drive — Award-winning Indianapolis Noir by Ian Woollen.

Strands of the Web: Short Stories of Harry Stephen Keeler — Edited and Introduced by Fred Cleaver.

Suzy — A collection of comic strips by Richard O'Brien and Bob Vojtko from 1970.

Tales of the Macabre and Ordinary — Modern twisted horror by Chris Mikul, author of the *Bizarrism* series.

Tenebrae — Ernest G. Henham's 1898 horror tale brought back.

The Amorous Intrigues & Adventures of Aaron Burr — by Anonymous. Hot historical action about the man who almost became Emperor of Mexico.

The Anthony Boucher Chronicles — edited by Francis M. Nevins. Book reviews by Anthony Boucher written for the *San Francisco Chronicle,* 1942 – 1947. Essential and fascinating reading by the best book reviewer there ever was.

The Best of 10-Story Book — edited by Chris Mikul, over 35 stories from the literary magazine Harry Stephen Keeler edited.

The Black Dark Murders — Vintage 50s college murder yarn by Milt Ozaki, writing as Robert O. Saber.

The Book of Time — The classic novel by H.G. Wells is joined by sequels by Wells himself and three timely stories by Richard A. Lupoff. Lavishly illustrated by Gavin L. O'Keefe.

The Case of the Little Green Men — Mack Reynolds wrote this love song to sci-fi fans back in 1951 and it's now back in print.

The Case of the Withered Hand — 1936 potboiler by John G. Brandon.

The Charlie Chaplin Murder Mystery — A 2004 tribute by film scholar, Wes D. Gehring.

The Chinese Jar Mystery — Murder in the manor by John Stephen Strange, 1934.

The Compleat Calhoon — All of Fender Tucker's works: Includes *Totah Six-Pack, Weed, Women and Song* and *Tales from the Tower,* plus a CD of all of his songs.

The Compleat Ova Hamlet — Parodies of SF authors by Richard A. Lupoff. This is a brand new edition with more stories and more illustrations by Trina Robbins.

The Contested Earth and Other SF Stories — A never-before published space opera and seven short stories by Jim Harmon.

The Crimson Query — A 1929 thriller from Arlton Eadie. A perfect way to get introduced.

The Curse of Cantire — A classic 1939 novel of a family curse by Walter S. Masterman.

The Devil Drives — An odd prison and lost treasure novel from 1932 by Virgil Markham.

The Devil's Mistress — A 1915 Scottish gothic tale by J. W. Brodie-Innes, a member of Aleister Crowley's Golden Dawn.

The Dumpling — Political murder from 1907 by Coulson Kernahan.

The End of It All and Other Stories — Ed Gorman selected his favorite short stories for this huge collection.

The Fangs of Suet Pudding — A 1944 novel of the German invasion by Adams Farr

The Ghost of Gaston Revere — From 1935, a novel of life and beyond by Mark Hansom, introduced by John Pelan.

The Gold Star Line — Seaboard adventure from L.T. Reade and Robert Eustace.

The Golden Dagger — 1951 Scotland Yard yarn by E. R. Punshon.

The Hairbreadth Escapes of Major Mendax — Francis Blake Crofton's 1889 boys' book.

The House of the Vampire — 1907 poetic thriller by George S. Viereck.

The Incredible Adventures of Rowland Hern — Intriguing 1928 impossible crimes by Nicholas Olde.

The Julius Caesar Murder Case — A classic 1935 re-telling of the assassination by Wallace Irwin that's much more fun than the Shakespeare version.

The Koky Comics — A collection of all of the 1978-1981 Sunday and daily comic strips by Richard O'Brien and Mort Gerberg, in two volumes.

The Lady of the Terraces — 1925 missing race adventure by E. Charles Vivian.

The Lord of Terror — 1925 mystery with master-criminal, Fantômas.

The N. R. De Mexico Novels — Robert Bragg, the real N.R. de Mexico, presents *Marijuana Girl, Madman on a Drum, Private Chauffeur* in one volume.

The Night Remembers — A 1991 Jack Walsh mystery from Ed Gorman.

The One After Snelling — Kickass modern noir from Richard O'Brien.

The Organ Reader — A huge compilation of just about everything published in the 1971-1972 radical bay-area newspaper, *THE ORGAN*. A coffee table book that points out the shallowness of the coffee table mindset.

The Poker Club — Three in one! Ed Gorman's ground-breaking novel, the short story it was based upon, and the screenplay of the film made from it.

The Private Journal & Diary of John H. Surratt — The memoirs of the man who conspired to assassinate President Lincoln.

The Secret Adventures of Sherlock Holmes — Three Sherlockian pastiches by the Brooklyn author/publisher, Gary Lovisi.

The Shadow on the House — Mark Hansom's 1934 masterpiece of horror is introduced by John Pelan.

The Sign of the Scorpion — A 1935 Edmund Snell tale of oriental evil.

The Singular Problem of the Stygian House-Boat — Two classic tales by John Kendrick Bangs about the denizens of Hades.

The Smiling Corpse — Philip Wylie and Bernard Bergman's odd 1935 novel.

The Stench of Death: An Odoriferous Omnibus by Jack Moskovitz — Two complete novels and two novellas from 60's sleaze author, Jack Moskovitz.

The Time Armada — Fox B. Holden's 1953 SF gem.

The Tongueless Horror and Other Stories — Volume One of the series of short stories from the weird pulps by Wyatt Blassingame.

The Tracer of Lost Persons — From 1906, an episodic novel that became a hit radio series in the 30s. Introduced by Richard A. Lupoff.

The Trail of the Cloven Hoof — Diabolical horror from 1935 by Arlton Eadie. Introduced by John Pelan.

The Triune Man — Mindscrambling science fiction from Richard A. Lupoff.

The Universal Holmes — Richard A. Lupoff's 2007 collection of five Holmesian pastiches and a recipe for giant rat stew.

The Werewolf vs the Vampire Woman — Hard to believe ultraviolence by either Arthur M. Scarm or Arthur M. Scram.

The Whistling Ancestors — A 1936 classic of weirdness by Richard E. Goddard and introduced by John Pelan.

The White Peril in the Far East — Sidney Lewis Gulick's 1905 indictment of the West and assurance that Japan would never attack the U.S.

The Wizard of Berner's Abbey — A 1935 horror gem written by Mark Hansom and introduced by John Pelan.

Wade Wright Novels — *Echo of Fear, Death At Nostalgia Street, It Leads to Murder* and *Shadows' Edge*, a double book featuring *Shadows Don't Bleed* and *The Sharp Edge*.

Welsh Rarebit Tales — Charming stories from 1902 by Harle Oren Cummins

Through the Looking Glass — Lewis Carroll wrote it; Gavin L. O'Keefe illustrated it.

Time Line — Ramble House artist Gavin O'Keefe selects his most evocative art inspired by the twisted literature he reads and designs.

Tiresias — Psychotic modern horror novel by Jonathan M. Sweet.

Totah Six-Pack — Just Fender Tucker's six tales about Farmington in one sleek volume.

Trail of the Spirit Warrior — Roger Haley's historical saga of life in the Indian Territories.

Ultra-Boiled — 23 gut-wrenching tales by our Man in Brooklyn, Gary Lovisi.

Up Front From Behind — A 2011 satire of Wall Street by James B. Kobak.

Victims & Villains — Intriguing Sherlockiana from Derham Groves.

Walter S. Masterman Novels — *The Green Toad, The Flying Beast, The Yellow Mistletoe, The Wrong Verdict, The Perjured Alibi, The Border Line* and *The Curse of Cantire*. Masterman wrote horror and mystery, some introduced by John Pelan.

We Are the Dead and Other Stories — Volume Two in the Day Keene in the Detective Pulps series, introduced by Ed Gorman. When done, there may be as many as 11 in the series.

West Texas War and Other Western Stories — by Gary Lovisi.

Whip Dodge: Man Hunter — Wesley Tallant's saga of a bounty hunter of the old West.

You'll Die Laughing — Bruce Elliott's 1945 novel of murder at a practical joker's English countryside manor.

RAMBLE HOUSE
Fender Tucker, Prop.   Gavin L. O'Keefe, Graphics
www.ramblehouse.com   fender@ramblehouse.com
228-826-1783   10329 Sheephead Drive, Vancleave MS 39565

www.ingramcontent.com/pod-product-compliance
Lightning Source LLC
Chambersburg PA
CBHW030330020726
47493CB00004B/1228